GANG GIRL

Maria Gomez is fourteen years old and lives in the slum section of New York City called Spanish Harlem.

Her mother calls her "Trouble," because Maria hates most of the things that make up her life. She hates her bad-tempered step-father and she hates seeing her mother work slavishly scrubbing floors in other people's houses but most of all she hates the feeling she has that she is in a trap and will never be free.

By leaving her family to become a gang member, Maria does become free of many of the worries she had when she was home but she gains troubles and worries as well.

How Maria comes to see that there is more in life—even for her—than being a member of a gang, how she begins to find her way toward a happier future, and how she is re-united with her family, make for exciting, true-to-life reading.

BONNIE
PONY OF THE SIOUX
THE JUNGLE SECRET
NORTH POLE: The Story of
  Robert Peary
BASEBALL BONUS KID
CAROL HEISS: Olympic Queen
GREEN LIGHT FOR SANDY
SEA TREASURE
THE BLOOD RED BELT
KENDALL OF THE COAST
  GUARD
RODEO ROUNDUP
NANCY KIMBALL, NURSE'S
  AIDE
FOOTBALL FURY
CIVIL WAR SAILOR
DINNY AND DREAMDUST
AUSTIN OF THE AIR FORCE
THE LONG REACH
FOOTLIGHTS FOR JEAN
BASEBALL SPARK PLUG
RUNAWAY TEEN
LIGHTNING ON ICE
HOT ROD THUNDER
JUDY NORTH, DRUM
  MAJORETTE
DIRT TRACK DANGER
ADVENTURE IN ALASKA
CLIMB TO THE TOP
FISHING FLEET BOY
JACK WADE, FIGHTER FOR
  LIBERTY
THE MYSTERY OF HIDDEN
  HARBOR
SCANLON OF THE SUB
  SERVICE
A SUMMER TO REMEMBER
NAT DUNLAP, JUNIOR
  "MEDIC"

BLAST-OFF! A Teen Rocket
  Adventure
TWO GIRLS IN NEW YORK
THE MYSTERY OF THE
  FLOODED MINE
CATHY AND LISETTE
EVANS OF THE ARMY
HIGH SCHOOL DROP OUT
DOUBLE TROUBLE
PRO FOOTBALL ROOKIE
THE MYSTERY OF BLUE STAR
  LODGE
ADVENTURE IN DEEPMORE
  CAVE
FAST BALL PITCHER
HI PACKETT: Jumping Center
NURSE IN TRAINING
SHY GIRL: The Story of Eleanor
  Roosevelt
SKI PATROL
BIG BAND
GINNY HARRIS ON STAGE
GRACIE
THREE CHEERS FOR POLLY
SECOND YEAR NURSE
THE BIG WIN
THE MYSTERY OF THE INSIDE
  ROOM
ARTHUR ASHE: Tennis
  Champion
THE MYSTERY OF THE THIRD-
  HAND SHOP
GOING, GOING, GONE
THE KID FROM CUBA: Zoilo
  Versalles
ROAR OF ENGINES
TV DANCER

GANG GIRL

by H. Samuel Fleischman

ILLUSTRATED BY
SHIRLEY WALKER

Doubleday & Company, Inc.
Garden City, New York

Library of Congress Catalog Card Number 67–17269
Copyright © 1967 by Doubleday & Company, Inc.
All Rights Reserved
Printed in the United States of America

Prepared by **R** Rutledge Books
First Edition

CONTENTS

Chapter One

WHAT'S THE USE?

"Hey, Maria, stop staring out that window. Come and help me with the cleaning. You know I have more to do than I can handle myself . . ."

"In a minute, Ma." Maria did not turn her head.

"All I've got is trouble. Trouble and children, and they are just more trouble . . ."

Maria let her mother's voice wash over her, not listening to the flow of complaints. Cleaning, cleaning —that was all her mother ever did—cleaning for other people, cleaning for her own kids. Maria wasn't going to look old the way her mother did, from cleaning other people's dirt!

Maria rested her elbows on the window sill and

stared down at the street below. Men stood around the front stoop of her apartment house, laughing, drinking beer. Some were in under shirts: it was a warm day in May. A group of boys were playing wall ball against a building.

Maria couldn't really remember living anywhere else. She only had little flashes of the way things had been back in Puerto Rico . . . the street they had lived on, with trees and grass—much nicer than the street they lived on now, almost as nice as some of the best streets here in New York. And she remembered her father.

"Hey, Maria. You trying to fall out the window?"

Maria looked down at the sidewalk a floor below. Her friend Dolores was standing there. Maria must have been day dreaming. She hadn't even seen Dolores come down the block.

"Dreaming of Carlos, I bet." Dolores grinned up at her.

"You just shut up, girl," Maria cried. Carlos lived next door, and Dolores knew Maria liked him. Dolores had no business shouting it out on the street.

"Come on down," Dolores said, laughing. "The girls are meeting over on the corner—114th and Lenox. Come on."

Maria hesitated a minute. She and Dolores had been friends as long as Maria could remember, but lately Dolores had changed. She was using lipstick and eye shadow, wearing her clothes much tighter, and going around with an older group of girls. It made Maria feel out of things.

"Maria," her mother ordered, "you stay right here and help me do this work." She was standing leaning on her broom, staring hard at Maria.

Maria looked down at Dolores and shook her head.

"See you around, kid," Dolores said, and she was off, swinging down the street with a walk that somehow looked too old for her. They were the same age, 14, but Maria knew that she was prettier than Dolores. She was taller, and had a better figure and she had nicer hair. If only Carlos . . .

"Maria!" Her mother's voice had a sharp ring to it. "You come here and help me this minute!"

Maria turned slowly and took the broom her mother held out to her. She knew what her mother was so angry about—she was afraid that Maria was going to join the gang, the Spanish Ladies, that Dolores belonged to. Well, why shouldn't she? At least they had some fun.

Slowly Maria swept at the dust on the floor. Her mother had gone into the kitchen. There seemed to be no end to the dust and dirt and cleaning—and all they had was two rooms and a kitchen. Her mother worked her knees off scrubbing people's floors, and what did it get her? Two dirty rooms and a kitchen!

Maria remembered what Mrs. Moore, her teacher,

had said to her one day. "Maria," Mrs. Moore said, "you are a very bright girl. You be sure to stay in school." Even the kindergarten teacher she had when she first came to New York from Puerto Rico had remarked that Maria had learned to speak English faster than anyone else in her class.

Mrs. Moore had told Maria that she could make something of herself if she tried, that things were not as bad as she thought.

But what was the use of working hard and doing well in school? After she got out of school, all she could get would be some job like cleaning floors. Once she had even told Mrs. Moore that she wanted to be a nurse some day. "Why not?" Mrs. Moore had said. "Nursing is a fine career for a girl."

"But fat chance of that ever happening," Maria thought now. "Nursing school and all those pretty uniforms—things like that cost money, and how could I ever make enough?"

Maria found herself staring out the window again. Why was she always doing that? It was as though she were trying to escape. But escape to where? She had never known a single person who had moved out of this neighborhood.

She thought of Luis Alvarez. Luis had been one of the toughest boys on the block until he came back from that reform school. Now he was different—going to regular school every day, dressing like some kind of college kid. Someone had even said he had a part-time job at night, so that he could earn the money to send himself through college. Luis had turned into a real hard-working square—and for what? What would it get a Puerto Rican to be a "nice boy?"

Maria quickly began sweeping again as Mrs. Gomez came back into the room with a pail of soapy water and a brush, and started scrubbing the floor where it had been swept.

"Where did you think you were going with that girl Dolores?" she asked. "I told you I didn't want you hanging around with her."

Maria looked at her mother, bent over, washing the floor. "My friends are my own business," she answered.

Her mother stopped scrubbing and turned to look straight at Maria, her face sad. "I know. That's what I'm worried about. I don't mind Dolores. It is that gang of girls she hangs around with. I've heard people talk. Those girls are wild. They run around with the gang that Carlos belongs to. I don't know what's going to happen to you, Maria, if you start going with them." She turned back to her work, shaking her head.

"What else can I do for fun?" Maria demanded, "—wash floors?"

"Don't speak to me like that, girl. I do my best for you."

Maria didn't answer. What was the sense? Her best! Four kids—and she couldn't even keep her own husband, Maria's father. Maria didn't know why her father had left. It had been a long time ago, a couple of years after the family had come from Puerto Rico, when she was five. She remembered him, though. Brown and thin, with slick black hair and a scratchy black mustache. He used to laugh with her a lot and tease her. Then, when she was about seven, he just wasn't there any more. That was when her mother had gone to work as a cleaning woman. And after a while, Alberto had appeared—and how Maria hated him!

"Mama, Mama. Chico's teasing me." Rosa, Maria's five-year-old sister, was standing in the door way, pouting.

"Rosa, don't be such a *niñita*," Mrs. Gomez said, rising slowly from her kneeling position. "And, Chico, leave your sister alone." Eight-year-old Chico dashed past Rosa, pulling her hair, and ran into the other room.

"Where's Juan?" Mrs. Gomez called after him.

"Out following your man Alberto around somewhere," said Chico.

"Don't you talk to me like that, Chico. Maria, you finish doing these floors, while I start the cooking. Everyone's going to be wanting to eat soon."

"This is Saturday," Maria thought. "Alberto has money. He won't be back for any dinner."

Maria wasn't sure exactly why, but from the very beginning, when Alberto had first come to live with them, he had been mean to Maria—really mean. She guessed it was because he knew how she felt about him. But he wasn't her real father: why should she treat him as if he were? He didn't belong in their house.

Maria found herself wondering how Dolores's father treated her. She had a real father, although he wasn't around much. But Dolores never talked about him.

What were those friends of Dolores's doing now? "Something better than washing floors, I bet," Maria thought. Why had she been afraid to go with Dolores anyway? Those girls really had fun. Maybe Dolores had the right idea and Maria was silly to be a goody-goody stay-at-home.

"Well, well, look who is the new scrub woman around here!"

Alberto was leaning against the door way, a beer bottle in his hand.

Juan came from behind him into the room. "Leave her alone, Alberto," he said, flopping onto the couch and switching on the TV.

"I just mean I think she makes a *good* scrub woman," Alberto said, grinning, and sat down next to Juan on the couch. "Ah, what a home! A woman in the kitchen, a woman doing the cleaning. I keep telling myself what a lucky man I am."

Maria stood up, furious. "What right have you to talk to me like that?"

"I can talk to you any way I want. I'm your father, remember?"

Maria tried to hold back her anger. She knew Alberto was enjoying this, just as he always enjoyed getting her mad.

She usually managed to hide her feelings, but right now Maria felt that she had never hated anyone so much in her life. She didn't know why—Alberto had said worse things to her before. But suddenly everything seemed to be pressing in—her mother always sweeping at dirt that never seemed to go away, and the small crowded apartment, and Alberto!

"You are not my father," Maria heard herself shouting. "You are nothing like my father! He was nice, and you are no good. Get out of his house! Get out of my mother's house!"

"What is this all about?" Mrs. Gomez was standing in the door way to the kitchen, looking from Maria to Alberto.

"Your charming daughter is telling me to get out of the house," Alberto answered, grinning.

"That's right, Mama. Tell him he has to leave. Tell him he doesn't belong here." Maria was close to tears.

14

"But, Maria, of course he belongs here. He's the man in this house."

"Oh, Mama! No, he's not. Don't say that, please. Why do you let him stay?".

"Maria, I do it for you, for all my children." Her mother took a step toward her.

"For me! Oh no, Mama. Please, not for me." With a sudden sob, Maria ran to the door.

"Where are you going?" her mother asked.

"Out."

"Maria, don't be silly. It is time for dinner."

"I'm going anyway," and Maria turned, running out the door.

"Maria, come back!" her mother called, as she ran down the stairs.

And, from the street she heard Alberto's voice through the open window. "Oh, let her go. She's not worth worrying about so much."

Chapter Two

GIRL GANG

Maria ran down the block, past the dirty gray buildings, past men shooting dice on the sidewalk, past all the faces staring out of the windows. Music seemed to be coming from everywhere, from apartments, from the barber shops and record stores along Lenox Avenue, and it all made one big sound in Maria's ears as she ran along.

She liked the feeling of running, of going faster than anyone else on the sidewalk. It was like being free, as if she weren't tied down to the same slow pace as other people. This is what all those faces staring out of windows really wanted to do—get out and run!

Finally, Maria slowed down to a walk. This was the first time she had ever done such a thing—run out of the house that way. But now that she had done it, she was glad. Before, she had always kept quiet when Alberto started acting up, because she knew it made him mad. This time, she had probably done just what he wanted by running out of the house, but what did she care? She didn't have to sit still while he made fun of her.

For the first time in her life, Maria felt really in control of things. She wasn't afraid of Alberto any longer. She could do what she wanted. And Maria knew now what she wanted to do. She was going to find the gang, the Spanish Ladies.

She had come to the corner of Lenox and 114th Street, but Dolores and her friends weren't there. "Probably over at their hang out," she decided, and headed in that direction.

Man, wouldn't her mother have a fit if she knew that Maria was going over to be with those "bad girls?"

The Spanish Ladies' hang out was on 115th Street, in a building that had been half torn down and then left that way. As she approached, Maria looked up at the doors that had been used to board up the top floor of the building. Seeing doors like that always gave her a funny feeling—so many doors, going nowhere.

Maria smiled at herself. "Sure think you are a big brain, don't you, girl?" She picked her way through the mess that paved the way to the front door.

Maria knew most of the girls in the gang, but she had never been to their hang out before. Dolores had told her about it, but somehow, most of these girls had never been very friendly. They probably didn't think she was tough enough, or something.

Loud music was coming out of the room on the left. The hall was very dark, and Maria thought that she saw a rat running down it. Quietly she stood in the door way. She had never realized how many girls were in this gang. Some were dancing together; some were sitting on an old couch, or by the window;

others were leaning against the walls. And practically all of them were smoking cigarettes. The walls were dirty and bare, and plaster was hanging from them.

The girls all seemed to be having fun. They looked so free, Maria thought. There was no one yelling at them, giving them orders. They could do whatever they wanted. No wonder her mother didn't want her to come over here.

Maria suddenly felt very much alone, standing by herself in the door way. Nobody had even noticed her. She saw Dolores talking to a group of other girls, and walked over to her, trying to look as though she belonged here.

"Well, well," Dolores said, "and what ever took you away from mama?"

"Hi, Dolores," Maria smiled. "Mama has Alberto, remember?"

"Looks like you've finally caught on." Dolores smiled back.

The other girls started talking to Maria. They acted friendly enough. She knew most of them slightly from school—whenever they went to school. Looking around, Maria realized that most of the Spanish Ladies were the girls who cut classes as much as they could. Not one of them seemed to worry about doing her school work or doing any of the things that Maria had been taught were right. They just thought about having a good time.

"It would be fun to be like that," Maria thought. "It would be fun never to worry about anything, never have anybody at you all the time to do this, do that, clean the house, wash the clothes, get the supper. . . ."

"Who are you?"

Maria jumped a little at the deep voice close beside her. She turned quickly, to see a tall girl with broad shoulders standing there. She was pretty, and she wore a lot of eye shadow and lipstick. Maybe that was what made her look older and—well, somehow more sure of herself than anyone else in the room. Maria knew who she must be—Rita, the president of the Spanish Ladies.

"I'm Maria Gomez," she said.

"Well, what do you want here?" Rita didn't sound friendly. And she looked angry.

"Maria's a friend of mine," Dolores put in.

Maria noticed that the room had become quiet. Everyone was watching her, to see if she'd stand up to Rita.

"I was just . . ." she began.

"Hey!" One of the girls, standing by the window, turned back to the room. "Look smart, kids—here comes a bunch of the Pirates!"

At once, Rita lost interest in Maria. She hurried over to a broken piece of mirror that hung on one wall and studied her face in it. Maria watched her

smooth her hair, then take a lipstick out of her pants pocket and use it carefully.

Maria turned to the door way as a group of boys came into the room, laughing and singing. These were the Ebony Pirates, and the Spanish Ladies were their sister gang. Carlos, the boy who lived next door to Maria, was the war lord of the Pirates. That was an important job, Maria thought, watching him come into the room. In a way it was the same as being a general in the army. A gang's war lord made all the arrangements for fights with other gangs.

Carlos was taller than any of the other boys and he had a strong, hard face. He was the only boy Maria had ever liked. When they were little they had played a lot together, out on the front stoop or in the street. Once Carlos had taken her to the movies on 125th Street.

But now Carlos was one of the toughest boys in the neighborhood, and he seemed to think of Maria as a little kid. Sometimes, passing her on the street, he wouldn't even speak to her, as if she weren't worth bothering about.

But he spoke to her now. "Hey, Maria, what are you doing here?" He sounded surprised—and pleased. "I didn't know you belonged to the Ladies." For once, Carlos seemed to have all his attention on her.

Maria smiled up at him. "I'm not a member yet,

but I hope to be one real soon." She tried to look as sure of herself as Rita looked.

There! She'd said it. And now that she knew being a member of the Spanish Ladies would let her see Carlos often, Maria knew that she *did* want to be a member. She wanted it more than she could remember wanting anything for a long, long time.

"Hello, Carlos." Rita had come across the room and was standing next to him, her hand on his shoulder.

"Hi, Rita, baby."

Now, Maria felt, she might as well not have been in the room. All Carlos' attention was on Rita. He put his arm around her and smiled down at her in a way Maria had never seen a boy smile at a girl.

"How's my pretty girl? Say, don't you look fine! I like that blue stuff on your eyes. And that lipstick—!" Carlos finished the sentence by leaning over and kissing Rita on the lips.

When he raised his head, Rita began to laugh. "Come over here, you," she said, pulling Carlos toward the mirror. He looked at his face in the glass and grinned at the bright red smear of lipstick on his mouth.

"Doesn't look as good on me as it does on you," he said to Rita.

"And you know where that stuff comes from?" Rita asked. "Straight from the counter in the five-and-ten, and I didn't pay a nickel for it."

Carlos' arm went around her shoulders again. "I wouldn't expect you to," he said. "You're my girl, aren't you?" His arm tightened around her. "You're a cool one, Rita. You know just how to play it!"

Maria couldn't take her eyes off them. Would anyone ever act that way with her, so proud, so sure? Was there any chance that Carlos himself could ever feel about her the way he felt about Rita?

Rita grinned up at Carlos. "You bet I'm a cool one," she said. "You don't catch me playing it the squares' way—going to school, working for a few dollars, living in messy apartments with a bunch of screaming kids. That's not for little Rita! I can get more for myself—including money—without working and without the school bit. Rita lives cool!"

They started laughing together. Maria thought that she might as well not have been there. She looked around the room. Everywhere, boys and girls were laughing and talking to each other. Even Dolores had a boy with her. Maria had never felt more out of it.

Well, she told herself, she wasn't going to be out of it much longer. She knew one thing for sure—she hadn't been lying to Carlos when she said she wanted to be a member of the Spanish Ladies. She did want to—more than she wanted anything in the whole world!

Chapter Three

A "LITTLE JOB" FOR MARIA

The next day was Sunday. What woke Maria in the morning was the sound of her mother and Alberto screaming at each other. This happened every week. Each Sunday morning they had a fight over whether Alberto would go to church. Maria's mother always wanted him to go with her—and she always lost the argument.

"Listen to them!" Maria said, under her breath. "Who needs it, all this fighting?"

"Maria! Maria!"

"Yes, Mama?" Maria didn't want to answer, but she knew her mother would keep on calling if she didn't.

Blairsville Junior High School
Blairsville, Pennsylvania

"Maria, get up and get breakfast for your brothers and sister while I'm at Mass. Come on, now, move along!"

Slowly, Maria got out of bed. She went out of the apartment and down the hall to the bathroom that served everyone on the whole floor, then came back and washed her hands and face at the sink in the crowded, tiny kitchen. She put cornmeal on to cook and, while it was cooking, she began to think ahead. As soon as Mama was home from Mass, she planned, she would go pick up Dolores, and the two of them would go to the Spanish Ladies' hang out. Maybe some of the Ebony Pirates would be there . . . maybe even Carlos. But even if he wasn't, Maria wanted to see Rita again. She had to find some way to get on the good side of the president, because by now Maria was determined that she was going to belong to the Spanish Ladies or die trying.

When the cornmeal was cooked Maria dished it up, poured a little molasses over the top of each dish, and called her brothers and sister to come and eat.

Fortunately, Alberto had gone out, so Maria didn't have to answer to his usual, "Where do you think you're going, girl?" She ducked out of the house and hurried off to pick up Dolores.

As they walked toward the Spanish Ladies' hang

out, Maria asked, "Do you think they'll take me, Dolores? Can I join the Spanish Ladies?"

Dolores shook her head. "Don't ask me—Rita's the one who decides. The rest of the girls are scared of Rita. They go along with anything she says. Me, too. I wouldn't tangle with that Rita for anything."

"What's she like?" Maria asked. "I mean, when you get to know her."

"Nobody really knows her," Dolores said slowly, "except maybe Carlos. Rita doesn't pal up with anybody. She's all by herself, Rita is. She makes her own rules, and those are the only rules she pays any mind. She's a—" Dolores hesitated, then went on— "oh, she's a funny one, all right. I don't know what to tell you."

"What would make her like me, do you know that?"

Dolores shrugged her shoulders. "Search me."

They walked the rest of the way in silence. When they got to the hang out, only a couple of girls were there ahead of them. But more came as time went by and finally Rita herself appeared.

She didn't seem any more friendly toward Maria than she had been yesterday. "What are you doing here?" she asked in that deep, hard voice of hers.

"I—I came with Dolores," Maria told her.

"You got no right here. I told you that yesterday. Get out of here, girl—this place is for the Spanish Ladies, and nobody else but!"

Maria drew a deep breath. It was now or never. "But that's what I want—I want to join the Spanish Ladies!"

"You got some nerve!" Suddenly Rita grinned. "And nerve is something I like. Listen, what makes you think you can be a Spanish Lady? What have you got to offer?"

Maria swallowed hard. "Just—just me," she said, in a small voice. "But Rita, I'll be a good Lady. I'll do anything you want me to do."

Rita's grin broadened. Her teeth were very big and white, and Maria thought she looked like an animal ready to take a big bite. "You bet your life you will—if we should decide to let you in. But first you got to prove you're fit to be let in to the Ladies."

Maria found that her knees had begun to shake. She hoped nobody would notice. "How?" she asked.

Rita walked across the room and threw herself down on an old couch that was propped up on bricks. "Well," she said slowly, drawing out each word, "that takes some thinking about. Let me just turn that over in my mind a little."

Maria wondered if it would be all right to sit down, too. She felt as if her legs wouldn't hold her up much longer. But she decided Rita wouldn't like that, so she stood in front of her, shifting from one foot to the other.

"Well," Rita said at last, "I guess we'll start out by

having you do a little job for me. You pick me up
something at the dime store—and baby, I don't mean
buy it!"

"You mean, steal it?"

Rita laughed. "I sure do. You ever stolen anything
before?"

"Oh, sure. Sure." Maria was beginning to feel a little
sick at her stomach. If only she could sit down!

"Okay, I got an idea. Tomorrow, you go to the dime
store and pick up some new blue eye shadow for me.
I'm running out."

Maria didn't answer. She could think of nothing to
say.

Rita gave her a quick, sharp look. "Well?"

"Y-yes," Maria managed to get out. "Sure. Sure I
will."

"All right." Rita leaned back a little. "You want to
be a Spanish Lady, Maria, you got to prove your right
to be one. Spanish Ladies have got to have class."

Dolores came across the room to stand beside Maria.

"She'd make a cool Lady," Dolores said. "I've known
her all my life."

"How come I've never seen her in Youth House?"
Rita wanted to know.

"She's too smart to get caught, that's why," Dolores
answered quickly.

Rita's eyes turned back to Maria. "So what have
you done that would make you a good member?"

Maria knew what kind of answer Rita wanted, and she gave it to her. "I've been stealing fruit from the corner store since I was four." She said it in a rush, hoping that would make it sound true. She had never stolen anything in her life, but she knew that was what most of the kids did.

"What else?" Rita demanded.

"And—and oh, stuff from the dime store and things like that. I—I've stolen so much I don't remember. I can do anything you want me to."

Rita grinned. "Okay, prove it. Get me that blue eye shadow tomorrow and—well, we'll see." She got up from the couch and walked out of the room.

Maria and Dolores looked at each other. "You going to do it?" Dolores wanted to know.

"I don't know," Maria said slowly. "I just don't know."

By the next morning, Maria did know. She had spent the rest of Sunday and all of the night—a worried, sleepless night—making up her mind. This was a turning point in her life, Maria knew that. She could obey Rita's order and get to be a member of the Spanish Ladies—and everything would be changed. Or she could not obey, and everything would stay just the way it was.

"I can't stand that," Maria had told herself, lying awake in the dark. "Things have got to change. I can't stand the dirt and the mess and Mama always at me, and Alberto always here, always making trouble. I can't stand things the way they are, and I'm the only one who can change them."

Next morning she went to school, but she might as well not have gone, for all the attention she paid. The only thing she could think of was when the 12 o'clock bell would ring . . . and her whole life would start to change.

At last the bell rang. Maria walked out of the school on stiff legs, and down Lenox Avenue to the dime store.

The store was full of people. Maria walked over to the eye shadow counter. Just her luck—a sales lady was standing right there!

"May I help you, young lady?" the woman asked.

"No, ma'am," Maria replied quickly. "I'm just looking."

Young lady! Oh boy, nobody had ever called her that before. Maria's mother used to call her "Chita" sometimes because she thought that Maria looked like a movie star from Puerto Rico. After Maria's father left, her mother usually just called her "Trouble." And that Alberto—he never called Maria by any name.

She moved slowly along the counter, waiting for the sales lady to turn her back. It was hard to pretend that she was looking at lipstick and perfume, and even harder to keep from staring at the sales lady.

31

"Something better happen pretty quick," Maria thought. It looked funny for her to hang around not buying anything. How had Rita managed it?

Just as she was deciding she had better leave, the sales lady finally turned to wait on a woman on the other side of the counter. Maria walked back toward the eye shadow.

"Keep cool," Dolores had said. "Take your time. Wait for exactly the right moment, and don't look nervous."

But Maria was nervous. She knew she wasn't supposed to be, but she couldn't help it. What worried her most were the other customers. It was supposed to be easier to steal if the store was crowded—that's what Dolores had told her, anyway. But what if someone saw her?

Well—Maria held her breath as she stood right in front of the eye shadow section—she couldn't be chicken if she wanted to be a member of the Spanish Ladies. And she wanted to be a member—she wanted Carlos to like her, and she wasn't going to scrub floors all her life!

"This is it," she told herself. There was only one woman looking at something farther down the counter, and the sales lady still had her back turned. The moment wouldn't last long, Maria knew. She had her eye on the package of eye shadow she wanted. She reached out her hand and picked it up. Then, glanc-

ing quickly around her, she dropped it into her pocket and started to walk slowly toward the door.

Well, that hadn't been so bad after all. And she had done it! She had lifted something straight under a sales lady's nose. Wait until she told Rita!

"If Carlos could only see me now," she thought. "I'm just as good a thief as Rita or any of the Ladies!"

Maria was just at the door when she felt a rough hand on her arm.

"Just a minute, sister!"

All at once Maria knew that this big man who had her by the arm must be the store policeman. The store policeman! Why, she had forgotten there was one! How stupid could she get? A cold feeling went all over her. She just couldn't get caught—she couldn't!

"Let go of me!" she cried. "I didn't do anything."

"What's that you have in your pocket?"

"Nothing. There's nothing in my pocket," she said, but the man held her tightly and pulled the box of eye shadow out of her pocket.

"I thought so," he said.

"Oh, that—I was going to pay for it. Honest I was."

"Sure, sure. That's why you walked right out of the door. Tell it to the judge," the policeman said.

"Judge? What judge?" Maria could feel the tears coming. But she told herself that she must not cry.

"Listen, girl—I am going to call a cop!"

Chapter Four

"I MAY DO
IT AGAIN . . ."

All through the time the dime store policeman was handing her over to the corner cop, with everyone staring at her, and all through the time she was being questioned at the station house, Maria felt nothing. The only thing she thought to do was not to tell where she lived.

"Gomez, Maria Gomez," a police woman repeated her name after her. "There must be hundreds of Gomez families in this neighborhood. What are your parents' names, child?"

Maria thought fast. "I don't have any parents," she answered. She didn't want Mama to hear about this.

She didn't want anyone to know about it. Alberto would beat her for sure if he found out.

"If you will only tell us who your parents are, you can go home and come back to appear before the judge tomorrow," one of the policemen said.

"I don't have any parents," Maria repeated.

"You must live somewhere, Maria," said the police woman.

"On the street."

So Maria was put in one of the little cells—almost like cages—for the night. After what she had heard from kids in the neighborhood, she was surprised to find that none of the police had laid a hand on her since she had been arrested. She had been sure that she would be beaten when they took her to the station house. The Ladies had even warned her about that. "Cops are mean. You be ready to just hang loose and protect your head so they can't hurt you."

But no one hit her. They gave her supper and she had a cot to sleep on.

Finally Maria let herself think about what had happened. What a mess! Her first little job, and here she was, probably going to jail. What would happen to her, anyway? She had never thought about being caught. She had just pictured herself telling Rita all about it, and how impressed Carlos would be. He would be impressed all right—with how stupid she was!

Caught by the store policeman! At this point, probably, the whole neighborhood had heard about it. How would she ever get into the Spanish Ladies now?

At least she had been smart about one thing—not giving her home address. Maria realized how frightened and worried her mother would be when she didn't come home tonight, but that was better than letting her mother find out where she was. And Alberto! For a minute she had forgotten about him. When Alberto heard about this, he'd use it against her, Maria was sure of that. He'd use it to show her mother what a bad girl Maria was, not worth worrying about. . . .

"Forget about Alberto," Maria told herself, but that was easier to say than to do.

She tried to make herself believe that sleeping in this cell was a lot better than sleeping at home, with all those kids sharing her room and with that man, that Alberto, in the next room. She wasn't ever going back to that apartment if she could help it!

But maybe she wouldn't even get the chance to go back. Maybe they would put her in jail. Maria wasn't so sure she wanted to spend time in prison, even though she knew it was the tough thing to do—even though it would mean that the Spanish Ladies would accept her.

She didn't really want to spend even this one night in jail, all alone, Maria admitted to herself. She almost

37

wished her mother were with her. She almost felt as if she were going to cry. But she wouldn't let herself cry. Spanish Ladies didn't cry. Spanish Ladies—why, they'd laugh at being in jail!

"Well," Maria told herself, "I want to be a Spanish Lady, so I have to learn to be tough. I won't know what's going to happen until tomorrow, so I might just as well get some sleep and stop thinking about it!"

"This doesn't look much like a court room," Maria said to the police woman who took her to the small, shabby room the next morning.

"Well, it is," the woman told her, pulling on Maria's arm to make her sit down on the bench beside her.

Maria looked at the group of men gathered in the front of the room before a high desk. Were they the men who would decide what was going to happen to her, she wondered.

Suddenly there was movement in the front of the room, and one of the men stepped forward and called out something in a loud voice. Maria couldn't make out the words.

The police woman tugged at her arm again. "Stand up, Maria," she said.

Everyone in the room stood up. A door opened. And then, to Maria's surprise, a tall, brown-skinned woman in a black robe entered the room and sat down on a chair behind the high desk.

"That's the judge," the police woman whispered.

The judge? "Well . . ." Maria thought, "imagine that—a lady judge. A *black* lady judge! Why, that lady is darker than I am! How did she ever get to be a judge?" Maria couldn't remember ever having known a black woman who wasn't cleaning someone's house, or waiting on tables, or maybe working in a beauty parlor or something like that. But a judge! Who did she think she was, anyway! What was she trying to prove?

The police woman pulled on her arm once more and Maria sat down again, but she couldn't take her eyes away from the judge. What did it mean to her that this judge was a Negro?

"Maybe it means she'll go easy on me," Maria told herself. But then she shook her head. "Probably not. Probably she'll be harder on me than a white judge would be. She'll think I'm a disgrace to her or something."

Maria remembered what Dolores had said to her once. "You can't make it the white man's way. That's not for you. They are just trying to keep you down. Don't play their game. Try to be smarter than they are."

Well, up in front of this court room was one black person who *had* made it some way or another. "How did she get there?" Maria asked herself. "How did she make it? She must have had pull—she'd never have made it without some kind of pull!"

A door at the side of the room opened and two armed guards brought in a thin, sick-looking boy. This was the judge's first case. Maria knew right away what he was here for—drugs. She had seen that kind of boy, with the gray skin, with the funny, see-nothing look in his eyes, standing on street corners . . . just standing there, swaying back and forth.

The judge looked at the boy for a long time without saying a word. Then she shook her head slowly and told the police to take him to Bellevue Hospital.

"That boy must have a twenty-dollar habit," the police woman whispered in Maria's ear.

"Man," Maria thought, "that means he has to buy twenty dollars' worth of drugs every day just to keep going! Carlos says he's tried that stuff. Wonder if he's ever going to have a habit as big as that?"

It frightened Maria to think that Carlos might turn out to look like the boy who was being led out of the room and to the hospital. Maria had no use for junkies, those people who took drugs.

"Gomez!" a man now shouted. "Maria Gomez."

"Go ahead." The police woman gave Maria a poke as she rose slowly and walked forward toward the judge. Maria felt all the eyes in the court room burning through her like little pins. Suddenly she

40

wanted to be four years old again, sitting on her father's lap, her mother cooking dinner in the kitchen. Things had been good then. She had known where she was, what to expect. Now she was afraid.

Maria stood before the judge, her head high. "Don't ever let on that you are scared," Dolores had told her once. "Just keep cool."

"Maria," the lady judge looked straight at her. Close up, she didn't look mean. "Maria, have you ever tried to steal anything before?"

"No, ma'am."

"Why did you take the eye shadow, Maria?" The judge looked almost sad.

"Because I wanted it." *Fresh*, that's what her mother would have said. Maria was just a no-good, fresh girl. But she couldn't tell the judge all about the Spanish Ladies and Carlos. Besides, it was true. She had wanted that eye shadow—she had *needed* it— and she didn't have the money to pay for it. She'd *had* to steal it!

"Are you going to steal anything again?" the judge asked.

What a strange question. Well, she didn't know, but she thought that she probably would. "I don't know," Maria answered.

The judge looked angry. "Now listen to me, Maria—" she began. Suddenly there was a movement at the back of the court room, and Maria saw her mother

41

walking quickly toward her, followed by Alberto. How did they know she was here? Someone in the neighborhood must have told them.

As they came up beside her, Maria's mother gave her a worried look. Maria turned away. She couldn't face her. She felt ashamed of what she had done and almost sorry for her mother.

"You are the girl's parents?" the judge asked.

"I'm her mother, Your Honor." Mrs. Gomez made a little bow. Suddenly Maria felt all the old anger at her mother returning. Why did her mother have to bow like that?

"Is Maria your only child?" the judge asked.

"No, Your Honor." Why did she talk like that? This lady was colored. She wasn't the landlord or the boss or anything. Maria hated to see her mother act so afraid. "I have three younger ones, Your Honor. Two boys and a five-year-old girl."

"And where do you live?"

"On East 111th Street," Mrs. Gomez answered.

The judge turned to Alberto. "What's your name?"

"Alberto, Alberto Valasquez."

"Do you support this girl?"

"I don't know anything about what she did. This girl, she is no good. I have nothing to do with her."

Maria sucked in her breath. She knew Alberto was mean. She knew he didn't like her. But to talk this way to the judge! She hadn't expected that.

42

"Is there a social worker assigned to this case?" the judge asked. A man looked at some papers and then shook his head. "That's too bad," the judge said. "We must do something about that. In the meantime, can I trust you, Mrs. Gomez, to be responsible for your daughter?"

"Yes, yes. She is really a good girl." Mrs. Gomez rocked up and down as she spoke, as if she were praying.

"Do you see that she attends school every day?" the judge went on.

"I do the best I can, Your Honor. I have to work, so the children take care of each other."

"She's no good, this girl!" Alberto burst out. "She hangs around with bad people."

"No, no," Mrs. Gomez cried. "She's a good girl. She's always been a good girl. I don't understand how. . . . But she will never do anything like this again."

"You know that's a lie, Mama." The words flew out of Maria's mouth before she realized what she was saying. Somehow she knew she had to tell the truth. "You know I may do it again."

"No, No!" Mrs. Gomez cried again, her face filled with fright. "That's not true."

If only her mother wouldn't be so frightened, Maria thought, maybe she wouldn't be acting this way herself!

"You see," Alberto put in, "I said she was no good."

43

"All right," said the lady judge. "All right, that's enough now. You two go and sit down."

Alberto and Mrs. Gomez went back and sat down.

"Come closer, young lady." The judge motioned Maria to come up to the high desk. "I want you to listen very carefully, Maria."

Maria frowned, and tried to keep her lips from trembling.

"You are only 14 years old and this is your first offense. You tell me you don't know whether or not you will steal again. Fair enough. If you do steal and if you do keep coming back here as you get older, you are going to end up in prison by the time you are 16. Do you understand that?"

"Yes, ma'am." Prison. Maria wanted to run away from those stern eyes. But she remained still and silent.

"And just to let you know that I mean what I say, just to give you a taste of what you may be heading for, I'm going to send you to Youth House for two weeks."

Youth House. *School for criminals,* the girls called it. The place where a lot of girls learned most of what they knew.

"Two weeks in Youth House," the judge ordered. Two weeks . . .

"I hope I never see you again in this or any other court, Maria," said the judge.

44

Never again.

"Next case!"

The police woman came forward and took Maria by the arm. She led Maria toward the side door, the same one the police had taken that junkie through. Maria swallowed hard. When she reached the door way, she turned for a moment to look back into the court room. Her mother was crying into her hand-kerchief. To Maria she looked like a little old lady. Alberto looked angry.

Maria turned and walked quickly out of the court room.

Chapter Five

"SCHOOL FOR CRIMINALS"

Youth House wasn't at all what Maria had expected. All the stories she had heard about it had made it sound like one big game, with the girls getting together to fool the guards and the social workers. "Like a vacation," Dolores had said.

It was no vacation for Maria. Most of the girls were, or seemed to be, older than she was. Not one of them was friendly to her when she was taken to the room that she shared with seven other girls.

When she stopped in the door way to look around, she was greeted by hard stares.

"Hello, Chita," the girl whose cot was closest to the door said in a mocking voice.

"My name isn't Chita," Maria answered.

"If you are Puerto Rican, your name must be Chita," replied the girl, a mean grin on her face.

"My name is Maria." Maria looked straight at the girl. She wasn't going to be pushed around so easily. Then two of the other girls began asking questions.

"Say, how come you speak English all right?"

"What are you in for, Chita?"

"For stealing," Maria said, crossing over to her cot and sitting down on it.

"What did you steal?" the girl on the cot next to her asked.

"A package of eye shadow," Maria said.

"Only eye shadow?" The girl laughed. "That's kid stuff. I broke a cop's nose."

"I stole a radio," another girl said.

Maria nodded. Everything was crazy, upside down. She felt very tired, though it was still morning. She lay down and closed her eyes, hoping that the girls would leave her alone. They did, beginning to chatter among themselves. Maria didn't listen. She felt so strange here. Stealing eye shadow—and getting caught at it, too! She almost laughed.

What did she want, anyway? There she was, telling the truth in front of a judge, getting herself put away in Youth House, and then finding she didn't feel so tough now that she was here. Maria opened her eyes and looked toward the small window in the wall. Some-

one had tried to make Youth House look less like a
prison, but all the windows were tiny and the frames
were made of solid steel.

Well, she was here, and she would have to make
the best of it. She pushed away the memory of her
mother's face in the court room.

Suddenly a bell rang loudly through the building.

"What's that?" Maria cried, jumping to her feet.
"Fire?"

"No, stupid," one of the girls said. "It is lunch—you
know, chow, food, grub."

She jumped up and changed quickly into the uniform
someone had handed her when she arrived at Youth

House. Then she followed the other girls out of the room as they lined up for roll call, then marched into the huge dining room. Rows and rows of girls sat on low wooden benches, while two dozen women with thick arms stood along the walls, watching. The room was noisy, hot, and filled with people.

Maria sat down and stared at the food on the long wooden table in front of her.

"What's the matter? Aren't you hungry?" a girl asked her. "Can't you appreciate good food when you see it?" Laughter went around the table.

The lumpy hash made Maria feel sick to her stomach. She drank some water and ate the dry bread. She felt as if she were going to smother in all the odors and noise. Eating at home, even with three young kids and Alberto, was better than this.

After lunch, all the girls were allowed to go to a large recreation room. A few played cards, and some of the younger ones were painting a big picture on the wall. But the older girls gathered in small groups, as though they were plotting something. Maria stayed by herself and tried to appear invisible. She wanted to be alone. She was afraid of the older girls, and what the younger girls were doing looked silly.

"Hey," yelled one girl from a group around a record player. "You want to dance?"

"No, thanks," Maria answered.

It seemed impossible to be left alone here. "You got any cigarettes?" asked a girl who couldn't have been more than 12 years old.

"No, I haven't," said Maria. "Sorry."

"Listen," the girl went on, in a low voice, "if you can get me some cigarettes, I can get you a uniform that fits you better. The lady that gives them out likes me."

"A uniform that fits better?" Maria asked, then realized the girl was right. Her uniform was much too big. But what difference did that make here? Some of the girls wore clothes that their parents had brought from home. Maria's mother hadn't had time to visit her, so she had to wear whatever they gave her. "This uniform is okay," Maria said.

"Well, if you can get hold of some cigarettes somehow, just look me up. My name is Sugar. Everybody knows me. See you around."

"See you," Maria replied, as the girl drifted off into the crowd of dancers. Maria wondered when her mother would come to see her, and if she would bring her some clothes. Or would her mother be too angry to come at all?

"Haven't I seen you around before?" A loud voice cut into her thoughts. Maria found herself looking up at a big Negro girl with a black scarf wrapped around her head.

"Maybe. Why?" Maria asked, not liking the expression on the girl's face.

"You look just like you'd belong to that Puerto Rican gang, the Spanish Ladies. Is that right?" The girl stared at Maria.

"What difference does it make to you?" Maria said. What did this girl want with her anyway? She looked as if she just wanted to pick a fight, and was going to do it no matter what Maria said. She noticed that some of the other girls had gathered around them.

"That's right. It doesn't matter to me if you say you are or you aren't, because you look to me like one of the Ladies. Do you know who I am?"

"No," Maria said.

51

"Well, my name is Gabby and I'm the chief of the Amazons!"

"I don't know about any Amazons."

"Oh, you don't. Well, Rita sure does. She knows a lot about the Amazons, little girl, and just to make sure you do, too"—Gabby took a step toward Maria, raising her open hand—"I want you to remember this."

Before Maria realized what was happening, the big girl struck her fiercely across the mouth. "And this . . ." Another blow knocked Maria back against the wall.

Gabby grinned. "That is just a sample of what is going to happen to Rita next week when I get out of here!"

Maria saw a police woman pushing through the circle of girls.

"What happened?" the police woman asked.

Maria trembled. She wasn't going to cry—not now or later!

"Nothing," she said, stepping slowly away from the wall.

"What's all the trouble about?" the guard asked.

"I don't know," Maria answered.

"Well, don't let me catch you in trouble around here again," said the police woman, walking away with a scowl on her face.

"Man, why did that girl jump on you like that?" It

was little Sugar, brushing off Maria's uniform. "What did you ever do to her?"

"Nothing." That was the truth. Maria had never even seen Gabby before. She had heard plenty about gang fighting, even about girl gangs fighting each other. But she never thought that she would ever be in such a fight. Or that she could be attacked right in the middle of Youth House!

"Say, you better have something put on that cut," Sugar told her.

Maria touched her cheek and felt warm blood.

"It was that big ring she wears," Sugar said. "That's what cut you. Come on. I know where to get you fixed up. Follow me."

Maria followed Sugar down the long hall to the nurse's office. While the nurse washed the cut and put a bandage on it, Maria found herself growing hotly angry.

"Okay," she told herself, "if that's how they want it, that's how it'll be. They want to be tough, they'll find out I can be tough, too."

The words sounded braver than she felt. The world itself was tough, all right. She was just beginning to learn how tough it really was. Well, then, she'd have to learn how to fight. She'd have to learn to give back the same as she got—from everyone, everywhere. That was the only way to get along. . . .

By the next day, with Sugar helping her, Maria knew

her way around Youth House pretty well. One of the things Sugar showed her was the room where the girls could go to meet their visitors, and in the morning Maria went there, hoping to find her mother. Instead, she found Dolores there, waiting for her.

"Hi, kid," Dolores said. And then, "Man, what happened to you? You look kind of beat up." She stared at Maria's face.

Maria knew what she meant. She had seen her face in the mirror when she washed that morning—it was swollen, and black and blue around her mouth.

"I got in a fight," Maria told her. "Ever heard of a girl named Gabby? She said she was chief of the Amazons."

Dolores nodded. "I've heard of her, all right. And from all I hear, she's murder! Is she in here?"

"Yes, she's here. She thought I was one of the Spanish Ladies. Before I knew what was happening, she hit me."

"The Amazons and the Ladies aren't very friendly."

Maria didn't need to be told that. "How did you know I was here?" she asked.

"It's all around the neighborhood. Everybody's heard about your little job at the dime store."

"I didn't pull it off. I got picked up," Maria reminded her.

"So what? I think it's made Rita change her mind about you. Listen, Maria, maybe it's a good thing this

54

happened. You can learn a lot in here. When you get out of here, Rita will have more respect for you. You keep your eyes and ears open, and pick up all you can. Try to find out what you can about the Amazons— what plans they have, stuff like that. Rita will be glad to hear anything you can learn."

"I'll try," Maria promised.

"But keep clear of that Gabby—she's pure poison!" Dolores got to her feet. "I'll run along now, but I'll be back to see you again, Maria."

Maria caught her arm. "Have you—I mean, have you happened to run into Mama on the street?"

Dolores shook her head. "No. Haven't seen her. Why?"

"Oh, nothing."

"You want me to go see her? You want me to tell her anything?"

"No. Forget it."

But Dolores seemed to guess what was in Maria's mind. "Maybe she'll come to see you tomorrow," she said, as she left.

But Maria's mother didn't come the next day, either. She didn't come any day that week. Every night, Maria told herself she didn't care. Then every morning she looked through the glass into the visiting room to see if perhaps this day, at last, her mother had come. But she was never there.

"All right," Maria told herself, "so that's the way it

is. Well, why waste time? I might just as well try to learn all I can while I'm here, the way Dolores told me to."

She found it was really easy to talk to the girls in Youth House. Sit down, smile, ask a nice, friendly question—and you had a new friend.

"Who's your boy friend?" a girl with dark eyebrows and very blond hair asked Maria one evening.

"I don't have one—not a real one," Maria answered.

"Oh, sure you do. Everybody does," the other girl said, smiling at Maria.

"Well . . ." Maria drew a deep breath and heard herself describing Carlos. "I—I like him a lot," she finished. That, at least, was the truth.

But the fact was that she had never had a boy friend—except for Carlos when she was a little girl, so long ago it didn't count. Since then Maria had always been afraid of boys. She had seen how Alberto treated her mother. Here in Youth House, though, it was different. The girls thought you were crazy if you didn't have a boy friend. Each of the girls seemed to have one of her own, and it made Maria feel left out.

"That's the trouble with me," she told herself. "I don't belong anywhere, with anyone. Mama doesn't even care enough to come here to see what's happened to me. That's why I want to be one of the Spanish Ladies—I want to *belong*. And I want a boy friend all my own, too, like the other girls. I want Carlos for my boy friend—and maybe, when I get out of here, I'll have a chance with him."

The girl with the blond hair went to play Ping-Pong with some friends, and another girl sat down in her chair. "You belong to a gang?" she asked. "I belong to the Sisters."

"I belong to the Spanish Ladies," Maria said, before she could stop herself.

Fortunately, the bell that meant they must go back to their rooms for the night rang just then, in time to keep the other girl from asking any more questions.

"I've got to watch myself," Maria thought, as she walked toward the big room she shared with seven other girls. "Somebody's going to catch me in a lie and then I'll be in more trouble than I ever imagined!"

Still uneasy, she undressed and got into bed.

One of the other girls came over and stood looking down at her. "You want some soda?"

Maria sat up. "Now? The door is locked. Pretty soon they'll be turning out the lights. How are you going to get soda at this time of night?"

"Easy," the girl said. "Come on."

Maria got out of bed and followed her to the door. There the girl took some playing cards out of her pocket. She bent two cards and slipped them into the space between the door and the lock. "Move them around a little"—Maria heard a click—"and slip the lock. See?" Minutes later they all had soda and crackers stolen from the kitchen.

All day and all evening, Maria was learning—much more than she had ever learned in so short a time before. Every day except Saturday and Sunday, she went to classes with all the other girls. It was just like going to school on the outside, except that here in Youth House you couldn't cut classes if you felt like it. But Maria had never minded school too much, and here it helped to pass the time. Outside school hours, there was the latest slang to be picked up, even the right way of walking and talking. Maria had always been a "good girl," just as her mother had said in court—going to school most of the time, coming home after school to help around the house. She had stayed off the street and away from the gangs like the Spanish Ladies until just a little while ago.

But no more, she told herself. From now on, things were going to be different. And here was the place to learn. . . .

"You've got to learn how to use your hands," Sugar told her, one day. "You don't have to let anybody slap you around. You can learn to protect yourself and fight back. Like this . . ."

Maria watched and listened and learned. She learned how to hide small things in her clothing and to keep an eye out for the guards while a girl broke into the kitchen. She learned how to play dumb—pretend she couldn't speak much English—if a guard happened to come along during the break-in. She learned how to "ring a register"—steal money from the cash register at a five-and-dime store. And she learned how to fight with finger nails, feet, and teeth.

The second week in Youth House passed swiftly. Maria told herself she no longer cared whether her mother came or not. She was beginning to like some of her new friends. The only problem was what she was going to do when she got out. She couldn't go back to the old life—home, and school, and being a good girl. Besides, why should she go home if her mother didn't even care enough to come to see her once? And home just meant Alberto and more fights.

On her last morning at Youth House, Maria found Sugar and said good-by.

"See you on the outside, Maria," Sugar said sadly, "if they ever get through giving me those tests. You know, I'm beginning to believe they are right. Maybe I am crazy or something. My mother always said so."

"You aren't crazy," Maria said. "See you soon."

They gave her back her street clothes and a dollar to get home with. "Home," she muttered. "Some home!" But as she went out the front gate and into the street, Maria found herself wishing her mother would be at the door to meet her.

No one was there.

Maria looked up and down the street, but didn't see a familiar face.

"Maybe they didn't know I was getting out today," she thought. But she knew that the Youth House people always told parents when their children were going to be released.

"Okay," she said, fingering the dollar bill in her pocket. "I can make it. I can make it alone. . . ."

A voice interrupted her thoughts. "Can I walk with you?"

Maria turned to see a young woman standing beside her. She was older than Maria, but the same height, the same coloring, and neatly dressed.

"What do you want?" Maria asked, not feeling very friendly. This woman must have been waiting for her. Who was she?

"Nothing at all. I just want to talk to you," the woman answered, smiling. Maria didn't smile back. "What are you, some kind of policeman?"

"No. I'm from the Youth Board. Your mother asked me to come."

Her mother! Maria didn't know whether to feel good or bad. At least her mother hadn't forgotten about her. But why hadn't she come herself? Too much trouble?

Maria said nothing. She just started walking down

the street. She didn't care if this woman had been sent by her mother—what was she to Maria?

But the woman followed her, keeping step at her side.

"My name is Helen," she said.

Chapter Six

JUST A DO-GOOD SOCIAL WORKER

"So you are from the Youth Board," Maria said over her shoulder. "What do you want with me?"

"I told you—your mother asked me to come." The woman followed Maria up the street and down into the subway station.

"Want an ice cream sandwich?" the woman asked, putting some coins in a machine as they got off the train at 110th Street.

"No thanks," Maria said. She stopped on the platform. Which way should she go now? She felt cold and hungry. She had no extra clothes, no place to sleep, and 80 cents in her pocket. Maria had that feeling of being lost that she had had in the court room.

"How about some lunch?" Helen asked, walking up the stairs.

Maria paused for a moment, then replied, "Sure, why not?"

Helen took her to a place for lunch, where Maria realized for the first time just how long it had been since she had eaten a good meal. "Okay," she thought, ordering a hamburger and fruit and salad and cake, "the lady wants to treat, let her treat."

Helen was silent as they sat together. She just smiled at Maria, watching her gulp the food in front of her.

Finally she said, "I've heard the food at Youth House isn't so hot."

"That's the truth," Maria replied.

"But it is healthy, they say."

"Sure."

Helen sipped her coffee for a moment.

"About your mother," she began. Maria didn't look up. "Alberto wouldn't let your mother go to visit you or even write to you at Youth House. He said that you'd got yourself into trouble, and it was up to you to get yourself out of it." She waited until Maria looked up at her. "I guess you and Alberto don't get along very well."

Maria smiled to herself. She wasn't going to tell

this social worker anything more than she already knew. She didn't see why her mother couldn't have come to Youth House. Alberto didn't own her!

"Don't be too hard on your mother," Helen said. Maria jumped. It was almost as if this woman had read her thoughts.

"It is very difficult for her to go against Alberto's wishes," Helen went on. "She feels that she needs him. It is hard on a woman with kids not to have a man around, and he does help support you and the other children."

Maria didn't say anything. If Helen was trying to defend Alberto, she had nothing to say to her.

"Don't think just because your mother didn't come

to see you that she doesn't care about you. She's very worried about you. That's why she wanted me to talk to you," Helen said.

"Say, how do you know all this, anyway?" Maria burst out.

"The court assigned me to your case," Helen answered.

"My case? Oh, I see. I'm a case now. Well, what are you going to do about my case? What did they tell you to do to me?"

"Nobody wants to do anything *to* you, Maria. I just want to help out any way I can. But nobody's going to try to make you do anything." Helen's voice rose a little. "You know, nobody's making you sit here and talk to me. You can leave any time you want."

Maria didn't say a word. She just kept her head down and ate her lunch.

"What are you going to do now?" Helen asked.

"I don't know," Maria said.

"What about school? You are planning to keep on, aren't you?"

"That's a drag. It doesn't get you anywhere," Maria answered quickly.

"I know that Youth House can give a girl a lot of tough ideas," Helen told her. "But try to get anywhere without school, Maria, just try it. I've seen your school records. . . ." Maria looked up in suspicion.

"That's right," Helen went on. "And you know what

I've learned, Maria? I've found out that you are a pretty smart girl. You have a good mind. But I don't have to tell you that. Your teachers have been telling you that for years. Now it is time for you to do something about it."

"For instance?" Maria asked.

"I'm not here to live your life for you, Maria. You know very well what you have to do—go back to school. Work. What about your wanting to be a nurse?"

"Well . . ." Maria began.

"Isn't it true?" Helen continued. "You know you wanted to be a nurse. Well, be a nurse, then! Lots of girls make it." Helen put her cup down.

"And what about money?" Maria's voice got louder.

"Work after school! That's the way to earn money. You are young. You've got lots of time, lots of energy. Oh, I know it isn't easy . . ."

"How do *you* know?" Maria asked.

"I know— But look at Luis Alvarez. Since he got back from Warwick a year ago, he's been working nights. Once he was war lord of the Ebony Pirates. Now he's planning to go to college when he finishes high school."

"Luis Alvarez, he's such a goody-goody, he makes me sick. Maybe he doesn't have two brothers and a baby sister sleeping in the same room with him. Maybe he doesn't have a mother with a man like Alberto in the next room. And if I did make some money, do you think they'd let me keep it? Do you think they'd let me save it, so I could be a nurse?" Maria knew that she was sounding sorry for herself. But just the same, it was true. She had been right when she had decided you couldn't make it that way. There were too many things against you.

Helen didn't say anything for a while. "Cigarette?" She held out the pack to Maria.

"I don't smoke."

Helen lit a cigarette, smoked it for a while, then quickly put it out. "Let's get out of here. Are you finished?"

"Yes, thank you."

They left the drug store and walked east on 115th Street. It was a bright day. The streets were filled with women shopping, mothers wheeling carriages, people out for an afternoon walk.

"Let's take a walk, Maria. Do you have a few minutes?"

"Are you kidding?" Maria almost laughed. "Time is the one thing I've got most of."

They walked slowly through the streets, leaving 115th Street and going down Fifth Avenue. Here it was noisy and there were more people—women on the front stoops, men playing dice games on the sidewalk. Children ran, screaming, through the parked cars, dodging the traffic in the street, bouncing balls against the steps of buildings.

"This neighborhood is so alive," Helen said.

"I hate it," Maria answered. The air smelled of garbage and fried food, mixed with the odors of fresh fruit and vegetables sitting in open carts. The smell of cheap wine came from the bottles that were passed from hand to hand along the street.

"Listen," Helen began. The sound of a drum came from an open window. In a minute it was joined by a guitar, and then a trumpet. Two little boys on the sidewalk began to dance to the music. "Where else could you hear that?" Helen said, smiling.

They crossed Lenox Avenue. Here the city had torn down several blocks of old buildings and built some nice low-rent apartments.

"Look at that," Maria said. "We were on a list to get in there, but they never called us. I guess my family isn't good enough."

"Nonsense," Helen replied. "There were thousands of people who wanted those apartments. The city could take only the very poorest families. Besides, I don't know if you'd like living with so many people. Some of the old houses are really nicer if they are kept up. There's a feeling of one big family in the older neighborhoods."

"One big family!" Maria repeated, and stared at Helen. "You know what I think? I think you are crazy. Sure," she went on, "you are a nice, do-good social worker. Mister Charlie, your big white boss, pays you to come up here and keep us quiet. At night, you can get away from this place and go home. You say you like it up here—the music and dirt and people—but you can go home at night. You don't have to live with it all the time."

"No," Helen said quietly. "No, Maria, you have it all wrong. I live in this neighborhood, just three blocks from where we are right now. I was born in Harlem Hospital and I have lived here all my life. I don't go away at night. I want to make it better, to help my people make it better."

Maria was surprised and ashamed. She couldn't think of anything to say.

"Listen, Maria," Helen said, "why don't you come

home to your place with me now? I know you probably don't want to go back there because of Alberto, but if I come with you, maybe it will make things easier."

"No, I—" Maria began.

"Hey, Maria. I've been looking for you." It was Dolores.

"Hi, Dolores. Long time no see."

"I was just over at Youth House," Dolores said. "I didn't know you were getting out so soon. Hey, come on. I'm going over to see the Spanish Ladies. Now that you've been in Youth House, they'll think you are hot stuff. Let's go!"

"Wait!" Helen cried. "What about going home? You haven't seen your mother."

"See you around," Maria said, running off with Dolores.

Chapter Seven

GANG GIRL

"Is she one of those social workers the court assigns to you?" Dolores asked, as they walked along.

"Yeah—trying to reform Maria before she really goes wrong." Maria laughed.

"Well, how was Youth House? Man, you must have learned a lot!"

Maria thought about it a minute. "I did. When I went into that place I was just a kid." She smiled at Dolores.

"Say," Dolores said, "that Gabby's been spreading the news about your fight all over. She still thinks you are a Spanish Lady—she's been boasting about how she beat you up."

"She beat me, all right," Maria said. "She sneaked up on me. But it will be different next time!"

"Say, that place really did change you." Dolores laughed. "I never heard you talk so tough before."

"One thing I did learn—the rest of the world is just like Youth House. Nobody is going to make things easy for you. If you want something, you have to go after it the hard way," Maria told her.

"Boy, wait until Rita hears you talk. You'll get in to the Ladies easily now," Dolores said.

"You think so?" Maria asked eagerly.

"You've got it made. Maria, you were lucky to get caught. It is better than if you had managed to get away with it."

Maria laughed. They walked along in silence for a moment. Then Dolores asked, "How did your mother and Alberto take it? I mean, weren't they awful mad?"

"I don't want to talk about it," Maria said sharply, without looking at Dolores, and Dolores didn't say another word.

It was funny, Maria thought. Dolores had always been the one with more experience, but now Dolores was looking up to her. Dolores was a member of the Ladies but she had never been in Youth House.

That social worker had tried to make Maria believe that she would be happier if she stayed in school and went home to Mama. Some chance! Maria was doing fine—in her own way!

They had reached the Spanish Ladies' hang out, and the two girls started up the steps. Maria had a nervous moment, thinking back to her last visit here, but then she remembered that she was a different girl now, and she walked into the house holding her head high.

"Hi, Dolores," a girl greeted them. She was sitting in a chair, smoking a cigarette.

Maria looked around the room. There weren't many girls there, but then, it was still early. Some of them might still be in school. "School!" Maria thought. Why, she hadn't been there for two weeks now. She'd gone to classes in Youth House, but that was different. "I guess I must have meant what I told Helen about school being a drag." Maria smiled to herself. "I'm free now, really free!"

"Well, if it isn't our little thief come home."

Maria recognized the voice and looked up as Rita came across the room toward her. She didn't look as pretty as she had the last time, Maria thought. She looked messy, and her eyes were red. Maria wondered how somebody could change so much in two weeks. But in spite of her words, Rita seemed more friendly toward her.

Some of the other girls gathered around.

"We heard all about it. How did they treat you in Youth House?" a girl named Carmen asked Maria.

"Except for Gabby, and the food, it was okay." Maria laughed.

"Yeah," Rita said. "We heard what Gabby did. Thought you were a member of the Ladies, did she? Well, then, I think we should make you a member! What do you say, girls?"

"Fine with me," Carmen said.

"She must have learned a lot at that place, just the way you did, Rita," another girl added. "Sure. Let's count her in."

"All right, Maria." Rita grinned at her. "You are now a member of the Spanish Ladies."

"Gee, that's great," Maria said. She hadn't felt this happy over anything in a long time.

"We usually don't do things this way. We Ladies are a fair gang. We let everybody vote on a new member. But since you've already been fighting for us, well, I guess that makes you a special case."

"'Special case.' From a court case to a special case. That's the way things go." Maria smiled, and all the girls started laughing.

One of them handed her a bottle of soda. "Here's something to celebrate with," she said.

"Stick around until the rest of the gang comes. Then we will really have some fun," Rita said.

"Sure," Maria answered. She felt good. Rita looked on her as one of the gang. She was really a Spanish Lady now.

They sat down around the old, ragged couch—the biggest piece of furniture in the room—and talked. The girls asked Maria about Youth House, and she and Rita compared notes. Then Maria just sat back and listened while the girls talked on—about boys, and the Amazons, and who had been arrested for what. She didn't pay much attention. She just felt happy. "At last I belong somewhere," she was thinking. "I really belong!"

Finally, some of the girls started drifting home for dinner. "They still have places to go," Maria thought. "This is the only place I have now."

"Say, does anyone have any money?" Rita asked. "How about going out and getting us some chow?"

"Sure thing." Carmen stood up. "I still have 50 cents left over from the purse I took out of an old lady's shopping bag in the grocery store last week." She laughed. "Pretty good job, too."

"I've got 80 cents," Maria said. "Take it." Carmen thanked her and went out of the door.

Maria wondered if she'd ever be able to pull a job like that. Sure, she had learned some tricks in the last two weeks, but to steal a purse was another thing.

"Oh, so you are out on the streets, are you? Not going back to Mama?" Rita smiled.

"No, thanks," Maria said, shaking her head.

"Well then, how would you like a room mate?" Rita asked.

75

"What do you mean, room mate?" Maria looked at Rita.

"Me! That's what I mean—how about moving in with me, here?"

"You mean this is where you live?" It had never occurred to Maria that Rita lived right here in the Ladies' hang out. But why not?

Maria looked around the room. It certainly wasn't the most beautiful place in the world, but it was a lot better than a park bench. Besides, nobody here would ever tell her to scrub the floor or wash the dishes. She would be completely on her own.

On her own! Maria had a sudden moment of fright. She was on her own, all right—not a penny to her name and only the clothes she was wearing when they took her to Youth House. And what was she going to sleep on, she wondered, seeing only one couch.

"Sure, Rita, I'd love to." Maria said it quickly. It was better just to do things, not think about them too much. What did thinking get you, anyway?

"Where will I sleep?" she asked Rita, trying not to sound worried.

"Over there, baby." Rita pointed to an old mattress, that Maria hadn't even noticed, in one corner of the room. "The girls found it on the street last week. They picked it up for another place to sit, but it will do fine for a bed."

"Well," Maria told herself, "I can't be fussy. Besides, this mattress isn't much worse than the cots at Youth House."

"Hey, girls, come and get it!" Carmen was holding up a box of hot dogs and soda, which she had just brought in. Maria sat down beside Carmen at the small table by the window and started eating.

"Aren't you hungry, Rita?" she asked, when Rita didn't come over.

"Sure. But I will be even hungrier after a sniff of this." Rita pulled a little envelope out of her pocket and waved it around. Then she took some of the powder in the envelope and sniffed at it. She looked just like Maria's old grandmother taking snuff. But Maria knew that powder wasn't snuff—it was dope.

Now Maria knew why Rita looked so different. "You sure you should be taking that stuff, Rita?" she asked.

"Sure I'm sure," Rita said, and laughed. "It has *some* kick. You want to try it?"

"No, thanks." Maria answered. She had seen girls at Youth House take it, and she didn't like what it did to them.

Pretty soon Rita began to sway gently. Her head rocked back and forth, and every once in a while she would laugh. Maria looked at Carmen, but Carmen only winked and kept on eating, so Maria did too.

Soon the other girls started drifting back, and Maria forgot about Rita.

77

"Well, kid," Dolores said. "And how does it feel to be a Spanish Lady?"

How did it feel? "Great," Maria answered, telling herself not to think about it. That was the trick—no thinking, no wondering, just doing. Rita and the rest of the Spanish Ladies seemed able to do it—just live day to day, minute to minute, even, without ever thinking about the future.

Later that night, after all the other girls had left and she and Rita were alone, Maria lay down on her mattress, wearing an old night gown one of the girls had brought her. Someone else had given her a pair of pants and a sweater for tomorrow.

"The Spanish Ladies are being real nice," Maria told herself. "I've got a place to live. I have clothes and friends. Wouldn't Alberto be surprised if he could see me here!" Look out. There she went, thinking again. Soon she would be thinking of her mother, of her brothers and sister, of home. "No," she whispered out loud. "No, this is my home."

Finally, she fell asleep.

In the morning, Rita seemed to be over the effects of the powder she had sniffed. It was a beautiful, bright morning. The only trouble was that neither of them had any money.

"That's no problem," Rita said cheerfully. "Let's go out and get some."

As they walked down the block, Maria was feeling

good. The whole day stretched ahead, with nothing she had to do, no one yelling at her. It was the first time she had ever waked up feeling free.

"There's what we are looking for!" Rita nudged her.

Maria saw an old lady walking slowly down the other side of the street. No one else was on the sidewalk.

"That's our breakfast," Rita said. "You catch her attention. I do the rest. Meet you back at the hang out."

Maria nodded. She thought she knew what Rita meant. She had heard at Youth House how it was done, but she still wasn't sure she could really do it. She tried not to act nervous. She had to show Rita— and herself—that she could handle things.

The girls crossed the street and approached the woman from behind. They kept laughing and talking to each other so that the woman wouldn't think they were paying any attention to her. Then, as they passed her, one on either side, Maria seemed to stumble and half fall against the woman. As she turned toward Maria in surprise, Rita snatched her purse, and both girls started running in opposite directions. As Maria dashed around the corner, she heard the screams of the old lady. Maria knew that there was no danger of the woman catching them, and she didn't see anyone else out on the street. She slowed down, and walked slowly back toward the hang out, one street away.

Rita was already there when Maria came in, empty-

ing the contents of the purse onto the couch. "Imagine," Rita said, laughing, "all that work for three dollars." She held the money up. "Well, at least it is enough to get us through the day."

Then she added, "You were cool, kid."

Maria smiled. She was pleased at Rita's praise, but now that it was over, she had a funny feeling in her stomach. Stealing from a person wasn't the same as stealing from a store. She couldn't forget the old lady's face.

"Well, how else are you going to feed yourself?" Maria thought. "Stop being so soft."

The rest of the day was like one long holdiay. Maria had never spent such a day before. Some of the other Ladies came to the hang out. Then they all went out and wandered up one street, down another. They didn't worry about a thing. They did whatever they felt like.

"Say, is this all the Ladies do—I mean just hang around and have fun?" Maria asked Dolores, later that afternoon.

"A good part of it is." Dolores smiled.

"Hey, do you know what these two Ladies did this morning?" Rita asked, coming over and putting her arm around Maria.

"No. Let's hear." Some of the other girls gathered around. Rita started telling about their robbing the old lady. Maria stopped listening. Everything was so different from the world that she was used to, where you went to school, washed up before dinner, mended your dress for the next day, and worried about your school marks. Would she ever really get used to this?

Suddenly, there was the sound of running outside, and a girl dashed into the room.

"Those dirty Amazons! Those thieves! One of them stuck a knife in my ribs and took my money—all I had. They are going to pay for that."

The girl's name was Olga, Maria remembered. She stood in the middle of the room and looked ready to cry. All the girls started talking at once.

"Those Amazons really think they are something."

"They get away with too much. We have to stop them."

"We have to show them that they can't do things like that to us."

"That's right," Rita said. "We've had enough. We've got to show those Amazons that they are dealing with the Spanish Ladies."

"But what can we do?" Carmen asked.

"How is this for an idea?" Rita said. "Suppose I challenge Gabby to a fair fight, just the two of us—tonight. What do you say, girls?"

"Right! Tonight!" Carmen shouted.

"Yes, yes," all the girls yelled.

"All right. Juana, you go make the arrangements—for tonight! At eight o'clock. Tell them they can't back out. The rest of you girls spread the word. And tell everybody to be back here by seven o'clock."

The girls went out, full of excitement.

Maria and Rita were left alone. Rita turned to her. "Well, Maria, this will be your first fight, won't it?"

Chapter Eight

FIGHT!

It was nearly seven o'clock. The Ladies were beginning to drift back into the club house in small groups.

Maria wasn't as excited as she had been earlier. She felt cold and scared. The last hour and a half she had spent with Rita hadn't been fun. As soon as the other girls left, Rita had taken the little envelope from her pocket. Shaking out the powder, she had begun to sniff it.

"Do you think you should do that now?" Maria had asked.

"Sure," Rita answered. "This is to get me ready for my fight with Gabby."

Maria decided to say something to the other girls when they came in. But none of them seemed to be worried about Rita. Maria cornered Dolores. "How is Rita going to be able to fight if she is taking that stuff?"

Dolores raised her eyebrows. "Rita is our president. If she sniffs that powder, it's her business." Maria didn't know what to say.

In the flickering light, Maria could see the brown, laughing faces of the Ladies.

"Okay, girls," Rita said, smiling in a strange way, "let's go!"

They filed out the door one by one, and down the stairs into the night. There were a dozen girls, all wearing red scarfs around their heads—the badge of the Spanish Ladies. Maria had one on, too. Most of the girls were dressed in tight pants and sweat shirts. Maria was wearing the sweater and pants that had been given to her the night before. Some of the other girls were wearing short skirts. One girl had on knee pads under her dress. "Just in case," she said. None of them carried weapons.

They moved quickly down the dark streets in groups of two and three. Maria caught up to Rita and walked by her side.

"How do you feel?" she asked.

"Oh, I feel fine, honey, just fine." Rita leaned against Maria as they moved down the street toward the park where the fight was to be held. "I feel just fine—riding high, flying, you know?" At the foot of the steps that led up to the rocks at the top of the park, Rita almost fell. Maria caught her quickly.

"Are you sure you want to fight?" she asked Rita.

"Sure, I'm sure," Rita said. She was laughing as the gang climbed the stairs.

The park was almost empty. It was the time when everyone was home eating supper. At the top of the hill the Amazons were waiting, already lined up along one side of a small cement square. They stood still, in a straight line behind their leader, Gabby.

"I was afraid you weren't coming," Gabby called from the center of the square.

"Well, don't you worry about that," Rita replied as the Ladies lined up behind her on the opposite side of the cement square.

"That Gabby sure looks mean," Maria thought, "—even meaner than when she beat me up in Youth House."

"All you spics are chicken!" Gabby yelled across the square.

Spics! If Gabby didn't look out she'd have all the Spanish Ladies to fight with. She was asking for trouble using that word in front of a Puerto Rican gang. Who did Gabby think she was, calling them spics, Maria thought in anger.

"Okay, nigger," Rita answered. "You just come over

here and see how chicken we are." *Nigger* was just as bad a word as spic, Maria thought. And besides, most of the Ladies were as dark as the Amazons.

Rita walked into the center of the square toward Gabby, and reached out to grab her shoulders. In a moment the two girls were down, rolling on the cement together, pulling each other's hair.

But after a moment it was easy to see that Rita was in no condition to fight. She couldn't seem to make her arms and hands do what she wanted them to. She kept grabbing empty air.

"Look out!" Dolores cried.

Rita wasn't really fighting back at all, Maria realized. Gabby quickly pinned Rita's arms and legs against the pavement and hit her in the mouth. Rita didn't move as Gabby sprang to her feet and stood over her body.

"So much for you Ladies. And don't any of you ever show up around here again. If you do, you will get the same—" Gabby drew her foot back as if to kick Rita in the head.

"No!" Maria cried out in horror. Now she was running forward, diving straight at Gabby, tumbling them both to the ground. Somehow she was pinning Gabby beneath her, hitting Gabby's head against the ground.

"There!" she cried, staring with wild eyes into Gabby's surprised face. "*That's* for Youth House, and *that's* for Rita, and *that's* for Helen, and *that's* for

Alberto, and *that's*—" Now the other Amazons were trying to pull her away from their leader.

"Enough. You win," Gabby cried. "I give up. Let me go!"

Maria allowed herself to be lifted from the ground, as the Amazons picked up their president and ran out of the square and down the steps.

Maria stood alone, catching her breath in the center of the little square.

There was a moment of surprised silence. Then Dolores ran shouting to wrap Maria in a powerful hug. "You did it! Maria licked Gabby. Good-by Amazons!"

"We beat the Amazons!"

"Did you see them run away?"

"Boy, you really pounded her, girl!"

All the Ladies gathered around Maria, slapping her on the back.

"You were great!"

"Really cool, kid."

But Maria didn't feel happy. She was tired and she felt sick from all the violence. She never wanted to be in a fight again as long as she lived.

"Rita was too far gone to fight," she said. "I took Gabby by surprise."

"Let's get out of here!" one of the girls cried.

In an instant the Ladies began to disappear into the trees, running down the far side of the hill.

"What about Rita?" Maria looked back at Rita, who seemed to be sleeping happily, a smile on her face. A little blood was running from one corner of her mouth.

"Rita is on her own now," Dolores said. "Come on. Stay here, the cops might come. You want to get locked up again?"

The two girls ran down the hill together, jumping over rocks, ducking under trees, tumbling swiftly down the slope and into the darkness.

Chapter Nine

A FINE CHICK

Maria opened her eyes and looked straight up into a blue sky. Where was she? She felt cold, hard metal beneath her. Frightened, she raised her head, and then she remembered. She was on the fire escape outside of Dolores's apartment.

Last night, after the fight, Dolores had invited her to spend the night at her place. Maria didn't want to spend the night alone at the Ladies' hang out, so she had come back here with Dolores.

Dolores had told Maria that she could sleep on the couch in their living room. Dolores's parents had three rooms and a kitchen. One bedroom was for her parents, and the other was for her older brothers. Dolores slept on the living room couch, usually. It wasn't big enough for both girls, so Maria had taken the cushions off the couch, and slept on the floor.

Maria fell asleep right away, but it seemed like only a minute later when she was awakened by somebody singing. A large figure had stumbled into the room, bowed deeply to her, and disappeared into the bedroom, still singing loudly. "Probably one of Dolores's brothers," Maria thought.

Dolores didn't wake up. She didn't even move. Maybe she was used to this. But to Maria it seemed as if the singing and banging around would never stop. So she had taken her pillow and blanket and crept out onto the fire escape. In spite of the cold metal beneath her, she had soon fallen asleep.

Now Maria just lay back, staring up at the blue sky. She pretended she was lying out on a big green lawn, with nobody around for miles. It was funny how you could make yourself feel you were all alone just by looking up at the sky. It was funny, too, Maria thought, that she usually never really looked at the sky. When you were down on the street, there were too many buildings and people. You never thought of looking up.

Maria wished she could just stay like this. She didn't want to think about last night, about the fight, about Rita. Everything had happened too fast. Only two days ago she had been in Youth House, wondering what would become of her. Since then, she had been made a member of the Ladies and had beaten Gabby, the president of the Amazons, in her first fight! Maria didn't know whether she was glad or not. It was almost as if she had no control over what was happening.

She stood up and stretched. It was still early morning. Only a few people were outside. Dolores's apartment was high up, so Maria could see over the roofs of the buildings across the street. She had never spent the night outdoors like this before.

"Hey!" Maria thought, and started climbing the fire escape to the roof of the apartment house. This was something she and Carlos used to do when they were kids. They would go up to the roof of his building and play, or watch the people on the street below.

Maria climbed onto the roof. It was a beautiful morning. She took deep breaths. The air seemed cleaner up here, fresher. Maria could see the East River. She stood watching the birds over the water, like little flying specks, and a tug boat moving slowly down the river.

"Maybe I can see my mother's apartment from here," she thought, and turned south. Dolores's place was on 112th Street, and her place was a block below. Yes, she could make out the roof of the building and the top floor. She wondered what her family was doing

now—if they were up, if Alberto had left the house yet. She felt like going over there.

"Oh, what do I care about them!" she told herself sharply, and turned away.

"Hey, Maria! Where are you?" she heard Dolores's voice calling out the window. Maria started to laugh. She must be giving Dolores a scare, seeing the blanket out on the fire escape and no Maria.

Maria looked over the edge of the roof. Sure enough, there was Dolores on the fire escape, peering around.

"Don't you ever think of looking up?" Maria laughed. Dolores turned a surprised face up toward her.

"What you doing up there?"

"Watching the birds, what else?" Maria started climbing down the fire escape.

"I know why you were sleeping out here," Dolores said. "It was that crazy brother of mine, wasn't it? But I'm used to him. Hey, what's wrong with your leg?"

Maria looked down and was surprised to see a long scratch on her leg. "That's funny, I don't feel anything. It must be from last night." She grinned at Dolores. "It is nothing—doesn't even hurt."

"Good," said Dolores. "Come back in the house now and let's get something to eat. Then we can go out."

They spent the day the same way Maria had spent the day before. She and Dolores just wandered around, doing what they wanted, not worrying about what they would do next. They walked into record stores, playing the records until the manager made them get out. They walked along the river. They stopped by the club house and talked to the other girls about the fight.

"I wonder what's happened to old Rita?" someone said.

"Maybe somebody found her—somebody like the cops. She may have to take a trip down to Lexington, Kentucky."

"What's that?" Maria asked.

"That's the place where they send dope cases. They keep them there for six months."

"Anyway, we beat the Amazons. Maria beat them for us!"

"Will we have to get a new president?" Olga asked.

"Yes," said Dolores. "Even if Rita didn't get caught, she'll never show up around here again, you can bet on that. I think we should elect a new president tonight."

That evening, all the Spanish Ladies gathered in the club house.

"Quiet, everyone," Dolores yelled above the noise. She seemed to be taking charge. The girls gradually stopped their chatter.

"Now, Ladies," said Dolores, "you all saw what happened to Rita last night."

"She couldn't fight at all," Carmen said.

"And you know why, too," Dolores went on. The girls looked at one another, but no one said anything. "Because Rita is a junkie, that's why." There were a few murmurs. "Rita's been no good for weeks. We can't afford to have a junkie for a president."

"That's the truth!" one of the girls yelled.

"Rita's out of the picture anyway," Carmen said.

"That's right," Dolores cried. "And I put up for president the girl who took over for Rita when she was too far gone to fight—the girl who fixed things so the Ladies can still hold their heads high, Maria Gomez!"

"Me?" Maria cried, surprised. "But I just joined the gang!"

"I know," Dolores said. "But last night you showed us what a fine chick you are. You can handle yourself. You would make just the kind of president we need!"

"Yes," Carmen said, "she sure handled herself last night!"

"And she beat Gabby," Olga put in.

Maria couldn't talk. She had never dreamed of becoming president of the Ladies!

"All right," Dolores said. "All those in favor of Maria as our new president say 'yes!'"

"Yes!" rang through the room.

"Maria," Dolores said, "you are the new president of the Spanish Ladies."

Chapter Ten

"WHAT DO WE DO NOW?"

"Everything is moving too fast," Maria thought.

"Well, Maria, what do we do now?" Carmen was asking her. Almost all the Ladies were at the club house this evening.

Carmen's question worried Maria. What was she going to do now that she was president, anyway? What had Rita done? What a crazy thing this was! She had just become a member of the Ladies.

"Why me?" Maria thought. "There are half a dozen others who would be better. Because I fought Gabby and won? But that's no way to choose a president."

"Why don't we have a party tonight? After all, we beat the Amazons, didn't we?" Dolores suggested.

There were cheers and shouts. Maria was swept along by the laughing group of girls.

"Hey, let's go out and get some food," someone shouted, and two of the girls started out the door.

"Maybe the Pirates will turn up," Carmen said.

The Pirates—Carlos, Maria thought. Maybe Carlos would come over tonight. What would he think of her now—president of the Spanish Ladies?

But the Pirates didn't show up at the club house that evening, and one by one the Ladies began to drift home. "Coming?" Dolores asked her.

Maria shook her head. "Not two nights in a row on the fire escape," she answered. "I'm going to stay here."

Neither the fact that she was alone nor the lumpy couch was enough to keep Maria awake. In the morning she woke to the smell of left over sandwiches and stale cigarette smoke.

She sat up on the couch. "Man, what a mess!" She looked around the room.

"Well, the first thing you have to do as president is to organize a team and get this place cleaned up," she told herself.

She began to laugh. Wasn't cleaning up one of the things she had said she would never do again? But then, look at the difference. Her mother was getting down on her knees to clean other people's floors. Maria was going to fix up her own club house because she was president of the Spanish Ladies! She began to feel better.

But she didn't have a penny in her purse. Her clothes were a sweater and pants one of the girls had given her. But what did she care? She would make a home for herself right here in the club house, and she wasn't going to worry from meal to meal!

Maria found it easy to go from day to day. One or another of the Ladies would bring clothes and sometimes food. And Maria was beginning to take care of herself. One afternoon she even managed to fill her pockets with fresh fruit. Another day she stole some change from the corner grocery store. "You can support yourself, Maria," she told herself. "You have it made."

She spent most of her time with Dolores, just having fun. She didn't worry about her family or about school. She wouldn't let herself think about what was ahead.

But she did have some worries. Like, why hadn't she seen Carlos? Why had the scratch on her leg begun to hurt? What was she going to do for clothes now. Sooner or later she might have to go to her house and get some. None of the girls really had anything extra to give her! Well, she would just have to do it when Alberto wasn't home.

"Wonder how he feels about me?" Maria thought. "He's probably mad because he can't get his hands on me. Wonder who he's being mean to now."

As for her leg, Maria kept hoping it was nothing. Besides, she didn't have any medicine for it, and she wasn't going to act like a baby and go crying to her mother.

One morning Maria walked out of the club house to find Helen standing there.

"Well, if it isn't the social worker!"

"Hello, Maria."

"You following me around? Well, you can just forget about this 'case.' I'm doing all right for myself."

"I know, Maria," Helen smiled. "I hear you are the president of the Ladies now."

"Who told you that? Have you been spying on me?"

"Sure, Maria. And I've got a policeman waiting around the corner to grab you."

Maria glanced nervously toward the corner.

"Honestly, Maria, you don't trust anybody, do you?" Helen gave a short laugh. "I know you are president because things get around in this neighborhood."

"You don't have anything on me anyway," Maria said quickly.

"How about that fight, Maria? And how have you been getting enough money to live on without a job?"

"Why don't you mind your own business," Maria snapped and started to walk away.

"Wait a minute, Maria! Are you too chicken to face the truth? I'm not a police officer. I'm not here to tell you whether what you are doing is right or wrong.

I just want you to be honest with yourself about it, Maria."

"Well?" Maria paused, looking at Helen. "I'm not too chicken to tell you that I've been living on my own, not asking anyone for anything. Sure, I've been stealing things. What have you got to say about that?"

"Nothing, Maria. What do you have to say about it?"

Maria didn't know what to answer. What did this woman want from her, anyway? Probably she still thought of her as someone to be "helped."

"Helen, you are wasting your time. I just don't see things your way, so save yourself a lot of trouble and go try to turn someone else into a square!"

"All right, Maria. I promise not to bother you again if you do one thing. Come over to the hospital with me. That leg of yours looks as if it could use some treatment."

"There's nothing wrong with my leg!"

"Oh, Maria, stop acting like such a baby. That cut needs care. What do you think, that the president of the Spanish Ladies is too big a person to have to worry about a cut on the leg? Come off it, Maria!"

"Well—" Maria said. The leg *was* hurting, and what did she have to lose? "Okay."

They began walking up Lenox Avenue, to the hospital. For a while, neither of them spoke. Then Helen said:

"I've seen your mother, Maria."

"Oh?" Maria was surprised. "You mean you have to keep in touch with the families of your cases, too?"

"No, Maria, I don't have to. As a matter of fact, your mother came over to see me at my home a few nights ago. I told you, I live in the neighborhood."

"What did she want to see you for?" Maria tried not to act interested, but she couldn't help asking the question.

"Well, you see, Alberto's gone, and she—"

"Alberto's gone! You mean he walked out?"

"That's not what I mean, Maria. He didn't walk out. She told him to leave."

"She did what!" Maria stopped dead. She couldn't believe what Helen had just said. Why would her mother, after all this time, decide to get rid of Alberto? She had never thought that her mother would have the courage to do such a thing.

"You can't understand why she did it, can you, Maria?" Helen had stopped, too. "It was because of you. She suddenly realized what having someone like Alberto around had done to you, and she decided to do something about it. But it is going to be awfully hard on your mother now, trying to support her children on what she makes. She is going to have to go on relief."

"What do I care about that?" Maria started walking again. "It has nothing to do with me." Her mother hadn't cared enough to come to see her in almost a month, had she?

"The reason your mother came to my house was to talk about you. She wants you to come back home," said Helen.

"Why doesn't she come to see me herself, instead of always crying to you for help?" Maria shot back.

"She's not crying for help, Maria. She's trying to do something that's hard for her, and my job is to talk to people who have problems like this. She doesn't want to ask you to come home until she thinks she can handle things. She doesn't want you to feel she'd like to have you home just so you can help out. She wants you to *want* to come home."

Maria didn't know what to say. Go home? She couldn't do that now. It was too late to go home as though nothing had happened. Besides, what would it mean? It would mean going back to school. It would mean getting a job, most likely. It would certainly mean Mama keeping an eye on her comings and goings, at her all the time about where she'd been and what she'd been doing. She didn't want any of that. She was way beyond that, now. Why, she was the president of the Spanish Ladies!

"Well, here we are, Maria," Helen said, as they entered the hospital. She took Maria into a room where her cut was treated. A girl about Helen's age was in the room, helping the doctor. She was wearing a crisp white uniform and a white cap with two high peaks.

"A nurse," Maria thought. "What's it take to be a nurse, I wonder. Graduating from high school, anyway, I bet. Well, that's not for me. Not any more."

"I want to look in on a friend of mine, Mae Kent, who's just had a baby," Helen said, when the doctor was finished. "Come along with me for a minute, will you?"

"Sure, why not?" Maria answered. It wouldn't hurt to get a look at more of the hospital, as long as she was here. She'd always wondered what hospitals were like.

Maria followed Helen into the elevator, and then along a hall and into a room with eight beds. Helen's friend was in the bed nearest the door.

"Hello, Mae," Helen said, leaning over to kiss her cheek.

"Hi!" Mae was sitting up in bed, and she looked very happy, Maria thought.

"Mae, this is Maria."

They said hello to each other, and then Helen asked, "How are you feeling, Mae?"

"Wonderful—just wonderful! I have two sons now, you know."

"They told me at the office. How do you and Joe like the idea of adding another member to the family?"

"Oh, fine. We were worried about the expense at

first. But now that Joe has bought out his partner, we own the whole place ourselves. Joe will make a go of it—I never have to worry about Joe."

Helen turned to Maria. "Mae's husband owns that store on 115th Street. You know, Maria—the store where Luis Alvarez works."

Maria didn't say a word. She could think of nothing to say. This woman, Mae, belonged to a different world from hers. A world where you never had to worry about a thing. She stood watching Mae's smiling face, feeling as if she could never understand people like these two.

"You know, Maria," Helen was saying, "Mae used to belong to a girl gang. What was the name of that gang?"

"Here it comes," Maria thought. "The case of the reformed gang girl."

Mae laughed. "We called ourselves the Rockettes. What an awful time that was. Am I glad to be out of that!"

"When I first met Mae she was on dope. You must have had a ten-, maybe a twelve-dollar habit by then, Mae."

"That's the truth," Mae agreed. "When I think of that. . . . Whew! It is hard to believe that was really me."

Just then Maria noticed a familiar face at the door,

wearing a broad smile. Then a lean figure walked into the room, carrying a big bunch of flowers.

"Luis!" Mae cried.

It was Luis Alvarez.

"Here are some flowers for you, Mrs. Kent. Hello, Helen."

"Oh, how pretty, Luis. Let's put them in water."

"He looks like a Boy Scout," Maria thought. But she had to admit that he wasn't bad looking.

"You remember Maria Gomez, don't you, Luis?"

"Maria!" Luis exclaimed. "I remember you as a messy looking little girl. You've grown up, Maria. How do you do?"

He shook her hand and made a funny little bow. "This is too much," Maria thought. She wanted to get out of this room, away from Luis, from Helen, from Mrs. Mae Kent and her new baby and her husband who owned his own store.

"Well," she heard herself saying, "I have to go now, Helen. See you around."

"Wait a minute," said Helen, as Maria edged toward the door. "What about your mother? I was hoping you . . ."

"Well, maybe I will go see her later. So long." With a quick glance at Luis Alvarez, Maria walked out of the room and down the hall.

"I could never stand being a nurse," she said to herself. "Uniforms, schedules, rules. And all that

school. Not me! I'm just not cut out for it. I'm a Lady."
She felt in her pocket for the red scarf. "The president
of the Spanish Ladies."

Quickly Maria wrapped the scarf around her head.
"They aren't going to change me the way they
changed Luis. No, sir. Free and easy, with no strings
attached."

At the main entrance to the hospital, Maria held the
door open for an old man in a wheel chair. Pushing
the chair was a nurse's aide, a young girl not much
older than Maria, in a bright yellow uniform and a
little yellow cap.

"Look at her," Maria muttered. "Little Miss
Stuck-up. Who paid for that fancy uniform, I wonder?
Sure, if I had the time and the money and if I wanted
to be a nurse, I could do it, too. Easy!"

Maria hurried out into the noisy street.

Chapter Eleven

WAR LORD

That night, Maria saw Carlos. He came over to the club house with half a dozen of the Pirates.

"Hi, Maria," he said, coming straight over to her.

"Hello, Carlos," Maria said, trying not to let her excitement show. This was the moment she had dreamed about, Carlos seeing her as president of the Ladies.

"I've been hearing a lot about you, Maria. Like you turned out to be some chick."

"I was lucky, Carlos." But she grinned.

"Some luck! I heard how you beat Gabby in that fight. I never would have thought you could do it." He winked at her. "How old are you now, Maria?"

"Fifteen," Maria said. She wouldn't be fifteen for months, but it sounded better.

"Well, you can tell your mother that you are growing up nice, real nice," Carlos said, looking her up and down.

"I won't be telling my mother anything," Maria said. "I don't need her, or an apartment full of screaming kids."

All of a sudden Maria felt kind of funny. That was exactly what Rita had said right here, only a little while ago. Was she going to end up like Rita? "That's silly," Maria told herself. "You can make it. Aren't you smart, girl? Isn't that what they told you in school? Isn't that what Helen said? You will never start sniffing dope. Besides, look at Carlos. He's war lord of the Pirates, and he's doing just fine."

Maria had heard stories about Carlos sniffing dope, and she noticed now how funny his eyes looked. But what did that matter? He was still the best looking boy Maria knew. If he was using the stuff, he could handle it.

Carlos drew her off into a corner. "Come here, Maria. I want to talk to you." He held her close to him. Maria smiled up at him. This time she was the girl he was interested in, the girl he was paying attention to. The war lord of the Pirates and the president of the Ladies—just the way it should be.

"Listen," Carlos whispered, "I got some business with you."

Business! That was not what Maria had expected.

"I want the Ladies to help the Pirates out—a real big job!" Carlos looked excited, and suddenly Maria realized that the way he was looking at her wasn't as though he liked her—it was as though he were giving her orders.

"What big job?" Maria asked, an edge of fear in her voice. She had been picturing for weeks how Carlos would feel about her now that she was somebody, but all he seemed to care about was that she was the president of a gang who could help him. Well, maybe if she could really help him, he would feel different.

"The Pirates are planning a big job. No more kid stuff—nickels and dimes and running numbers for a few bucks. We are going to stick up a store. There's real money there, Maria—hundreds, maybe thousands of dollars lying around by the end of the day!"

"Man!" Maria said. Carlos was right. This wasn't kid stuff. It was real crime—enough to get them all sent away for a long, long time.

"Maria," she told herself sharply, "that's no way for the president of the Ladies to be thinking. What are you, chicken? You were elected president for a reason —because the other girls thought you could handle things like this!"

"Where do the Ladies come in, Carlos?"

"It is simple. You girls watch out for the police, watch the store until we get there, then hide the goods while we disappear. You dig?"

"Sure, Carlos." They were to look out for the police, get there ahead of time to make sure there would be no trouble, take what was stolen and hide it after the Pirates had robbed the store. No, this sure wasn't kid stuff. But it was a test, Maria thought, a test of whether she deserved to be president of the Ladies.

"Listen. It is tomorrow night. I'm going to tell you where, but if you say a word to anybody, even one of the Ladies—"

Carlos didn't finish the sentence, but to Maria his face seemed changed—hard, mean. It was like seeing a stranger, not the Carlos she knew. Could this be how he really looked and she had never realized it before?

"I won't squeal, Carlos." She said it firmly because she knew it was true. But she felt nervous. It was hard to admit it to herself, but Maria knew she was afraid of Carlos.

"Good," Carlos said. "Just tell all your girls to meet here by nine o'clock tomorrow night. We hit the place at twelve, just before it closes, and I don't want your girls to have any time to talk before it comes off. We will give you your orders then."

"Whose store is it going to be, Carlos?"

"All right, if you want to know. But if anything goes

wrong, I will know who to blame. Joe Kent's place—on 115th Street."

"Joe Kent?" Maria had a sinking feeling in the pit of her stomach. "Isn't that where Luis Alvarez works?"

"That's right, girl." Carlos was smiling.

"But why there?"

"Because Luis is a square. He needs to be messed up. Somebody has to teach him a lesson, and the Pirates and the Ladies are going to do it! Remember—nine o'clock tomorrow night, Maria." And Carlos went off, leaving Maria standing alone in the corner.

It was almost 12 o'clock.

Maria stood in a dark doorway across from Joe Kent's store, trying to keep out of sight. The night was cool, with no moon, and strangely quiet.

Maria had just spent the most miserable 24 hours of her life. She thought she had finished with fear now that she was a Spanish Lady, but never before had she been so afraid. This was it, she kept telling herself. This was what being president of the Spanish Ladies meant. She had wondered what a president was supposed to do. Well, now she knew. It wasn't just making a home out of the club house or stealing a little money. It was leading her gang in a serious crime, robbing a store.

"Why is it so quiet?" Maria whispered to Dolores, who was flat against the door beside her.

113

"Those girls down at the corner must be keeping everyone out," Dolores answered.

Of course. Maria could see the two garbage cans that had been dragged out into the middle of the street. Members of the Ladies were also stationed at each corner to try to keep anyone from walking toward the store. Every girl had been told exactly what she should do.

Maria and Dolores were stationed directly opposite the store in order to take the guns and the money when Carlos and two other Pirates ran out the front door.

"You hide the stuff in your clothes," Carlos had told them at the club house earlier that evening, "so if anybody stops us there will be no evidence—nothing at all on us."

He had spent hours going over every detail with Maria and the other girls. Maria had said very little. She was too mixed up to know what to say. She had watched the other girls, to see how they took it. They had all seemed excited about the job. Were they just acting that way because they were afraid of the Pirates, Maria wondered, or because they wanted to appear tough? Or did they really get a kick out of the plan?

"You want a cigarette, Maria?" Dolores asked.

"No, thanks."

Dolores seemed surprised. "That's funny. Whenever

I feel bad or nervous, I just have to smoke. It makes me feel fine again."

"So Dolores must be scared about this too!" Maria thought. "Dolores," she asked, "have the Ladies ever done anything like this before?"

"Nothing this big. Not with guns," Dolores answered.

"Are you scared, Dolores?" Maria asked.

"Sure, Maria. Aren't you?"

Maria didn't say anything. So they were all scared! But what difference did that make? Nobody was going to do anything about it. It was as if they were all in some kind of trap, as though they had no control over what was happening. But what could they do? They were the Pirates' sister gang. It was up to them to help the boys out. "Besides," Maria had been telling herself all last night and all today, "this is what you wanted. You wanted to be tough—the president of the Ladies. Well, this is your chance to prove you can do it!"

But at the same time she kept on seeing the face of Mae Kent, and the tall, thin figure of Luis Alvarez. All day she had been thinking about them, and trying not to. She had thought about her mother, too—how she had sent Alberto away and how she would feel if she knew what Maria was doing. And about Helen . . .

"But what do they matter to me?" she thought. "The

Ladies are what matter to me now—and the Pirates. Stop being soft!"

So here she was. Across the street, in the store, she could see Luis Alvarez and Joe Kent stacking cans on a high shelf, as quiet and peaceful as could be. They didn't know that Carlos and two other boys were working their way along the back alley, getting ready to break in the back door.

"If I were just to tell them right now, warn them—" Maria said to herself. "But what are you thinking, girl! Would you tell on your friends? Let the police arrest Carlos, and all the Ladies, your pals? Are you going to squeal and get them locked up? You can't do anything now—you are in too deep!

Suddenly Maria felt like running. She didn't know where. Just to get away from here. To her father, somewhere. Even to her mother. Or to Helen. That was it. She would call Helen and Helen would tell her what to do. Helen cared about her.

There was a telephone booth on the corner. If she could just slip down there. . . . But how could she do that without being seen by Dolores and the other girls? And what could Helen tell her? And whom else could she call?

For the first time in years Maria felt like praying. But it wasn't any good. Nobody could help her. She had got herself into this mess. And she was in too deep to do anything!

Where was Carlos now? He must be about to break in. The boys had guns. What would happen?

Suddenly Maria found herself running across the street.

"Maria, what are you doing!" Dolores shouted.

"I've got to warn them!" Maria cried. She couldn't let this happen, no matter what. She had to stop it!

But just at that moment Maria heard the sound of splintering wood. It was Carlos breaking in the back door of the store.

As Maria ran through the front door, Carlos and the other two Pirates appeared at the rear entrance. They were holding small "zip" guns they had made themselves.

"Okay, everybody, flat on the floor!" Carlos cried, waving his gun at the direction of Joe and Luis. "What are you doing here, Maria?"

But before Maria had a chance to answer, Luis Alvarez sprang at Carlos, knocking the gun out of his hand.

The two boys struggled fiercely, finally crashing to the floor. A shelf filled with cans and jars fell down with a bang. There was the sound of glass breaking.

Joe Kent ducked behind the counter. The other two boys fired their guns and the bullets flew wildly around the room.

"Stop!" Maria cried. "Stop fighting! Stop shooting!"

Something shattered the front window of the store.

A pile of empty bottles crashed to the floor. Maria felt a sharp sting on the side of her neck as she ran forward and threw her arms around a boy just as he was about to hit Luis from behind. Luis had finally managed to pin Carlos to the floor when an alarm sounded in the street outside.

Everyone froze.

Luis jumped off Carlos, letting him rise to his feet.

"Okay, Carlos. You got off easy this time. Now beat it. And don't come back!"

The other two boys ran out the back door, but Carlos bent and picked up his gun and stood for a moment, gasping for breath. He stared at Maria, his eyes burning with hate.

"You. You tipped off the police, you dirty rat!"

"No, Carlos," Maria cried. "No, I didn't!"

A police car screamed to a halt outside. Carlos ran out the front door and down the street. Two policemen jumped out of the car, their guns drawn.

"Stop! Stop in the name of the law!" they shouted.

Carlos kept on running. He had almost reached the corner when he turned and aimed his zip gun at the police.

A single shot rang out, echoing like thunder against the cold, brick walls of the buildings. Carlos fell. He fell slowly, almost in slow motion, his head hitting the pavement with an awful thump.

Then there were screams and shouts and people

running all over the street, and more screams. Who was screaming? "It is me," Maria realized. "I'm screaming and I can't stop."

At last the screaming ended as Maria fell to her knees, her body shaking with sobs. She was crying. For the first time she allowed herself to cry.

Luis Alvarez knelt beside Maria, his arms around her, holding her head against his chest and speaking softly.

"Hey, now—there, there. Stop crying, Maria. Look, there's blood on your neck. You must have been hit by—no, it's a cut. There's a piece of glass in it. Let me see. There, there . . ." Luis held Maria close, rocking her in his arms.

"He's dead," one of the policemen said, coming back down the street to where Luis, Maria, Joe Kent, and a growing crowd of people stood in front of the store. "Killed leaving the scene of the crime. I guess he didn't know about your burglar alarm, Joe. Who's this, one of the gang?" The policeman eyed Maria.

"No, officer," Luis insisted. "She just happened to be in the store, a customer. She was cut by a piece of flying glass, that's all."

"Well, you better do something about that cut," the policeman said.

"Yes, sir."

"We don't want any more people getting hurt around here." The officer took off his cap, mopping the sweat from his brow. He was a big brown man with a tiny mustache. Maria thought he looked like her uncle in Puerto Rico. "Of all the crazy things to do," he said. "Why didn't that dumb kid just stop running?"

"You killed him!" Maria cried suddenly, sobbing again.

"Maria!" Luis said, wiping the tears from her cheek.

"That's right, young lady. I killed him. I had to. But I will tell you something. I know that boy. And he's been dying for a long time."

The officer turned away, got back into his car, and drove slowly down the street. An ambulance carrying the body of Carlos followed the police car, its red light flashing in the darkness.

Maria stood watching it disappear into the night. Then she started to walk away.

"Wait, Maria," Luis said.

"No, I've got to—" Maria began. But then everything seemed to fade away, the voices and the street and the night.

Maria had fainted.

Chapter Twelve

GOING HOME

Maria opened her eyes.

At first everything looked white: white walls, white ceiling, white railings on the bed. But gradually Maria could see figures lined up beside her bed. One, two, three, four. All different sizes.

It was her family.

Standing there straight as soldiers and all dressed up in their best Sunday clothing were Mrs. Gomez, Maria's two brothers, and her five-year-old sister, Rosa.

"Good morning, Maria," her mother said. "How are you feeling?"

And suddenly Maria remembered the night before.

She sat up quickly. "Why am I in the hospital?" she cried.

"It is nothing, Maria," Mrs. Gomez told her. "Don't worry. They told me it is not bad, but they want to keep you here until you get your strength back."

Maria felt the bandage along the side of her neck, and she began to remember. The big job. The police. Carlos dead. Everything spun wildly through her head as she sank back onto her pillow with a sigh.

Her mother and brothers and sister stood stiffly before her, the children shifting from foot to foot.

"Say hello to your sister," Mrs. Gomez told the children.

Maria turned her head a little and looked—really *looked*—at her mother. "She's beautiful!" Maria thought, and then smiled to herself. No, Mama wasn't beautiful. In fact, she hadn't changed a bit. She was still a small, dark, nervous-seeming woman, older than her years from hard work and heart break. But she was Mama—and oh, Maria was so glad, so glad to see her!

One by one the children came closer to the bed and stood looking at Maria with big eyes. "That's the way they'd look at a stranger," Maria thought. "I've been away so long. Or anyway, it seems so long!"

"Hello," Rosa whispered shyly. "Does it hurt?"

Then Juan put in, "We heard you were at that store when it got stuck up. It was a lucky thing you didn't get killed."

"Were you scared?" Chico wanted to know.

"I was scared," Maria told him. "Believe me, I was scared to death!"

"We came over to see you as soon as they'd let us," Juan told Maria. He reached out and touched her hand.

"How did you hear about what happened?" Maria asked. She was pleased that her family had come to see her, but she also felt very mixed up. A great deal of time seemed to have gone by, yet it was only last night that it had all happened, wasn't it? And how had she got here? And what had happened to the others—the Spanish Ladies, the rest of the Pirates? And Luis Alvarez . . . now she remembered his voice quieting her, telling her everything would be all right. But she could remember nothing after that.

"It was all in the papers this morning," her mother said. "Even your picture, with Luis Alvarez."

Chico laughed. "He had his arms around you, Maria!"

Maria felt her cheeks grow warm. "I must have fainted," she said.

"Your friend Helen came over and brought the paper," her mother went on.

"Helen?"

"Yes. She told us we could see you here in Harlem Hospital. It was Helen who asked the nurse if we could all come to see you for a minute together. Now, you kids go back out to the waiting room, the way you promised you would. I want to talk to Maria a little."

124

After Maria's brothers and sister had gone out, Mrs. Gomez said, "Maria, listen to me. I want you to hear my side of things, to—to help you make up your mind what you want to do now. When you started getting in trouble I—well, I realized how things had got to be the way they were, and I knew I had to do something. So—well, I think Helen told you. I told Alberto to go."

Maria started to speak. She realized how hard it was for her mother to talk this way. She wanted to say, "Never mind, Mama, it's all right now," but her mother held up her hand to stop her.

"No. Let me finish. It is hard to say but it needs to be said, Maria. I am sure you are angry with me for not seeing you for so long, but I could not see you until Alberto left. And then . . ."

"I know, Mama. I understand. I was angry and I was hurt. But it was partly my fault, too. We were—everything was mixed up. Whatever any of us did seemed to make things worse, not better."

Her mother smiled. "I know. But now I think things have begun to change. That Helen—she's some girl. She has helped me so much! She told me to apply again for city help to get a bigger apartment, and to speak to the welfare people, and how to get a better job. I made a list of everything, see?" Mrs. Gomez took a piece of paper from her purse and held it out to Maria.

"Anyway, what I want to say is, don't let the things you've done come between us. I mean, I hope you come back home. Don't feel that because you made some mistakes, you can't change. I used to feel that way, but it is not true. I want you to come home, Maria." Mrs. Gomez patted Maria's hand and smiled.

"I'm going to get the children to come back and say good-by," she said, and left the room.

Maria felt good. There certainly had been some changes. Her mother seemed so much happier, and she was being so nice and honest with Maria. Her mother really cared about her!

But her mother wasn't the only one who had changed, Maria thought.

When the family came back into the room to say good-by, Maria stopped them. "Wait a minute, everybody. I want to tell you something. No one asked, but I guess you are all wondering what I was doing in the store last night. The papers said I was a customer, right?"

"That's right, Maria," her mother said, "but you don't have to explain anything."

"But I want to, Mama. The truth is, I was there with the Spanish Ladies and the Pirates and Carlos"— it hurt to say his name, but she had to face it—"to rob the store. There was a plan. It was Carlos' idea, but I went along. I went along until it was time for Carlos and the two other Pirates to break in. Then I

knew I had to try to stop it. I didn't know what I was going to do—I just started to run across the street. I was too late to stop anything. I came in the front door just as Carlos and the Pirates came in the back way. That's how I got hurt." Maria touched her neck.

"Ahhh!" all three children gasped. To them it was like a thrilling story.

"What I'm trying to say, Mama," she turned to her mother, "is that you didn't have to ask me to come home. I hadn't realized it, but my mind was made up when I started running across the street last night. It was just so awful, I knew it was all wrong. And I knew that everything I had been doing was wrong for me.

"Mama, you didn't have to ask me. I'm glad you want me. I'm coming home."

"Maria!" Mrs. Gomez leaned over the bed and gave her daughter a kiss on the cheek. It was the first time she had kissed Maria in years. Maria saw that her mother's eyes were full of tears, but she didn't say anything.

"Maria's coming home!" The children gathered around her bed, laughing.

"The landlord had to go to court for not having enough heat in the building," Juan told her.

"How come I can't have a big bandage like that for my knee? Look at my scratch, Maria!" Chico cried.

Maria smiled. She knew how excited they were and she was pleased by the attention, but she felt tired now. She wanted to be alone. She had to think.

"All right, everybody," Mrs. Gomez said. "Time to go home. Maria has to rest. We are coming back to see her tomorrow."

As her mother was taking the children out, Maria asked, "How long will I be in here, Mama?"

"The doctor says a day or two at the most. They say you are weak—you have not been eating enough. They just want to make sure you are all right before you leave. Then you are coming home, Maria." Her mother smiled and walked out of the room.

"Coming home, coming home," Maria said to herself. She knew that everything she had told her mother had been true. She did want to go home, but something was bothering her. She felt very sleepy . . .

"Is she asleep?" Maria heard a man's voice asking. Who was that? Where was she? She opened her eyes to see Luis Alvarez standing by her bed. He had been talking to the nurse.

"Luis!" she said, trying to sit up.

"Easy, Maria." Luis smiled, pushing her gently back on her pillow. "How do you feel?"

"Fine. But Luis—I—" Maria suddenly felt very shy. "I was trying to warn you when. . . . If only I had . . ."

"I know, Maria. I know the whole story. It wasn't hard to figure out."

"And you still came to see me?"

"Why shouldn't I? Shouldn't I understand how you feel? I was war lord of the Pirates once, remember?"

"Yes." Maria smiled. "Luis, what made you decide to change?"

"Well, Maria." He smiled back at her. "I guess really the same thing that made you change your mind last night—realizing that the way things were going just wasn't good. That I was going to end up the way Carlos did, unless I did some pretty fast changing."

"Is it true you are going to go to college, and all that?" Maria asked him.

Luis started to laugh. "I don't know, Maria. I don't know what's going to happen. But it is worth a try, isn't it? Anything's better than the other way."

Maria lay back on the pillow and smiled. She felt peaceful with Luis sitting here next to her bed. It was funny how safe she felt.

But suddenly she thought of the Ladies, and Dolores, and Carlos, and everything came flooding back. "What happened to everyone, Luis? Did anyone else get hurt?"

"No, Maria. Only Carlos." A look of pain crossed his face, and then his expression changed. "Oh, I meant to tell you. I bumped into Dolores on my way in just now. You can imagine, she felt a little strange when she saw me. She had come to see you, but the nurse told her that you were asleep."

Dolores! Maria thought. And all the other Ladies—how were they? Was she still president? She found that she still cared about them.

"Luis," Maria said, "maybe the Ladies didn't like what happened last night any better than I did. Maybe we can have a different sort of club. Maybe—"

Luis was laughing at her. "Sounds like a great idea, Maria, but *maybe* you should get some sleep right now. You can't plan your whole life this minute."

"I guess I was sort of getting carried away." She smiled.

"Listen, Maria, why don't I come back and see you

tomorrow? I have to go to work now. The place is still a mess from last night. And if you aren't here tomorrow, I will go over to your house. Okay?"

Luis stood looking at her for a moment, then touched her hand gently and went out the door.

Maria looked at the empty door way, feeling very sleepy and very happy. The nurse came in and smoothed her sheets. "Well, maybe I can't plan my whole life this minute," she told herself, with a yawn. But as she settled back to go to sleep, pictures kept crossing her mind—Maria, president of the Ladies in a new, fixed-up club house . . . Maria as a nurse, smoothing the sheets for a patient. . . . Maria and Luis . . . She fell into a deep sleep.

Chapter Thirteen

A BEGINNING

Maria walked toward the Ladies' club house, a pile of books in her arms. It was a week after the job at Joe Kent's store, and this was the first time she had been back to the Ladies' hang out.

It had been a strange week for Maria. A strange and very happy one. After staying in the hospital for a few days, she had gone back to live with her family. And how different it had been! Her mother had tried to fix things up, with flowers and new curtains. Best of all, Alberto was really gone! And Maria had found a friend in her mother, someone she could really talk to. She had never dreamed that could happen.

So much else had happened—her going back to

school after all this time, and her friendship with Luis Alvarez—and it was all good. But somehow it hadn't been enough. Something was missing, and she knew what it was—the Spanish Ladies.

Sure, some of the girls had come to visit her in the hospital. She was still the president. But it was not the same. Since the night of the robbery, none of them quite trusted her. No one had asked her what had happened, but she knew they all were wondering.

That's why she had called for the meeting this afternoon. She was going to tell them what she had done that night and why she had done it. They would probably throw her out of the club. But, as Luis had said, there was no harm trying, was there?

When Maria reached the club house, she could hear the sound of voices. She walked into the room. It was filled with girls. Off in one corner Helen was standing quietly by herself. Maria had asked Helen to come to the meeting. She wasn't exactly sure why, but she felt that Helen would understand what she was going to try to do.

"Hi, Maria." That was Dolores. She was sitting on the couch with two other girls, but she made no move to get up. Dolores had come to see her at the hospital, but things were not the same between them. Would Dolores understand?

Suddenly, Maria realized that the talk had stopped

and that everyone was looking at her. "Hi, girls!" She smiled, and faced the room.

"Well, if it isn't our president," one girl said.

"Where have you been keeping yourself? Did you decide to stay away from us 'bad girls?'" another one asked.

"This is going to be harder than I thought," Maria muttered to herself. "Well, here goes."

"Girls," she began, "let's have a regular meeting. I've never done anything like this before, but I want things to run smoothly. Everyone will get a chance to speak."

Some of the girls laughed, but then the room became still again. Suddenly Maria felt very nervous. Looking into the waiting faces, she wondered what it really was she had to say to them. She had thought about it in the hospital, and afterward at home. She had found that thinking things out helped after all. If she could start the Ladies thinking, too—

"I have a question for our president."

It was one of the girls who had been stationed at the corner the night of the big job.

"All right, what is it?"

"Just exactly what happened the other night? I mean, before Carlos got shot?"

A stir went through the girls. Maria was sorry she had let someone else bring it up. She shouldn't have waited. But at least it was out in the open now.

"Wait a minute," Olga cried. "What about this social worker here? We can't talk in front of her. What's she doing here, anyway?"

"I asked her to come," Maria snapped. "We can say anything we want in front of her."

All the girls looked at Helen, but no one said anything.

"Well, Miss President, how about answering my question?"

Smart. These girls were smart, all right. Well, there was only one cure for it—the truth!

Maria took a deep breath and began.

"I ran across the street just before Carlos and the boys broke into the rear door of the store. I was trying to reach the store and warn Mr. Kent and Luis before the job began. I was hoping to stop the robbery."

A chorus of voices broke out.

"You rat!"

"Wait a minute, wait a minute!"

"Give her a chance!"

"Some president!"

Maria looked at Helen for support, but the older girl just stood silently, looking at her.

"Now we know why Carlos was killed!" Carmen shouted.

"There was a burglar alarm," Maria said. "As soon as they broke in the rear door a light went on in the police station. They never had a chance." The room became quiet again, as the girls listened. "You see," Maria went on, "the whole thing was dumb to begin with. It should never have been planned. And we shouldn't have had a part in it."

"But we are the sister gang of the Pirates. We are the Spanish Ladies!"

"That's right," Maria replied. "But if we had been half as smart as we think we are, we would have talked them out of it."

"That's easy to say now," Olga yelled.

"I know." Maria looked down at the floor. "I know. I didn't do anything to stop it. I know I'm partly to blame for Carlos' death. But"—she looked at the girls again—"so are we all."

No one said a word.

Then someone shouted, "I don't understand! You must be going soft or something. When we started this gang it wasn't supposed to be some kind of tea party. Now we've got a president who sounds like my old grandmother."

"Well," Dolores said, "you try and mess with our president. Have you forgotten what happened to Gabby?"

"The point is," Maria said, trying to make them understand, "that this *is* a gang. We *are* the Spanish Ladies, and proud of it. But it seems to me that we have to look out for ourselves better."

137

"But this is supposed to be a fighting gang!" someone yelled.

By now Maria was getting angry, too. "Fighting who?" she answered, raising her voice. "I will tell you. Fighting each other, that's who! And what's the good of it? Where does it get us? That's why I tried to stop Carlos. A thing like that had to end up with something bad, like Carlos getting killed. Why are we being so stupid? We are just hurting ourselves, getting arrested, or beat up, or strung out on dope, like Rita."

"Or getting hit by flying glass," someone shouted out.

"You can say that again!" Maria smiled, touching the fresh white bandage on her neck. If the cut had been an inch to the left, the doctor had said, Maria might have been killed.

She looked around the room. She had their attention now. They were following her, they were with her—at least for the moment. "Listen, we've got a good gang here. Let's do something for ourselves, instead of just doing what the Pirates tell us to do. Let's start thinking about things, making our own decisions."

"Like what?" Carmen asked. "Tell us about some of your big plans, will you? I think you are starting to sound like your friend here, this social worker. Next thing you will have us all out collecting old clothes for the poor."

"Hey, that's not a bad idea," someone cried. "I could use some old clothes myself."

Maria looked at Carmen for a moment. Then she spoke.

"I don't want to make the Ladies into a bunch of do-gooders. And I don't say we should start out having cake sales. But I do say we've got to do something. We've got to begin somewhere, all of us together— the Spanish Ladies."

"Do what, though?"

"What have you got in mind?"

It was Helen, moving a few steps forward, who answered the question. She spoke to all the girls, but her eyes were fixed on Maria.

"Well, to begin with, this place is a mess. This room, the club room of the Spanish Ladies."

"This building is going to be torn down by the city," one of the girls said.

Helen nodded. "I know. And there I can help you. There are many vacant places in the neighborhood— mostly stores—and some of the landlords are willing to let girls and boys use them to fix up a club house. The landlord has to know, though, that the people he lets use his place will take good care of it."

"How do you prove that?" Carmen demanded.

"If I believed you would take good care of the place, the landlord would take my word for it. And I think you could prove it to me."

There was a small silence. Then Maria asked the question she realized that none of the others could put into words. "Will you help us find a place, Helen?"

"Yes, I'll help you—if you'll make plans to have a nice, pleasant club house, a place you'll enjoy coming to, a place you'll be proud of and want to take care of." Helen leaned back against the wall again, her arms crossed, her eyes moving slowly around the room from face to face.

"It would be fun to have a nice place," somebody said.

"Sounds like a good idea." That was Dolores.

"It would be hard work," Maria said. She didn't want them to decide too quickly—and just as quickly forget about the promises they would have to make in order to get Helen's help.

"Hard work never hurt anybody!" Maria had trouble keeping from laughing, because Olga, the laziest of the Spanish Ladies, had said that.

All at once they were all talking:

"Say, my father works for an electric company. Maybe he could help us rig up some lights in the new place."

"I know a boy who is learning to be a carpenter at Trades High. I bet he could help us."

"I've got an uncle who works for a plumber."

"My mother would help us sew curtains and stuff, I know she would if I asked her."

140

"We could keep the place clean ourselves."

When the noise died down, Helen spoke again. "There are some things I can do, if you'll let me. For instance, it's fun to learn how to fix yourselves up. I could get a friend of mine who works in a beauty parlor to come and show you how to do your hair and put on make up. I could get another friend who works with me to teach you the latest dances, if you wanted to give a party."

"There's a lot we could do," Olga said. She sounded surprised, Maria thought. "There's a lot that I guess would be fun to do!"

"I'd like to learn to sew," Dolores said, suddenly. "Helen, do you think you could find somebody to teach us to sew?"

Helen nodded. "I certainly could. If I had a little time, I could probably find somebody who would give you an old sewing machine for the club house."

"It's working," Maria told herself. "Things are really starting to move."

But then Carmen raised her voice. "Oh, it all sounds fine, just fine," she said. "So you get yourselves a pretty place to come. Then what? You sit around and tell stories? You sit around sewing and fixing your hair? Not me! That's not my idea of a good time. Why, pretty soon you'll have a bunch of goody-goody kids trying to get in, and it won't be the Spanish Ladies any more at all!"

"You don't have to do anything you don't want to," Helen began. "But—"

"Wait a minute," Maria put in. "What's wrong with that? Maybe we could make our new club house a center for the neighborhood kids in the evenings. How does that sound?"

The idea caught fire. "We could have dancing to records," Dolores said.

"If we got a place with a kitchen, we could serve some food," Olga added.

They kept on talking for a while. Finally, Helen told them, "I have to go now, girls. But don't worry—I'll start first thing tomorrow morning to look for a new place for the Spanish Ladies to fix up for a club house." She waved to them, and went out.

"Ladies," Maria said, "the meeting is over. We have plenty to think about. Let's meet again tomorrow, same time, and make plans."

Suddenly Carmen broke in again. "Not me, I told you! I'm not coming back here tomorrow—or any time! I like things the way they are. If the Spanish Ladies are going to turn into a social club, count me out. Who's with me?"

For a moment no one answered. Then one girl came over to stand beside Carmen. Then a second came. Finally there were five of them, girls who had been silent most of the evening. Without another word, they marched out of the room.

"We won't miss them," Dolores said. "They would be trouble for us—trouble all the way."

Maria nodded. "I guess you are right. But—well, I thought maybe . . ." She shook her head. "I guess I'm lucky any of you want to stay with me."

After a moment, the girls began to leave.

"So long, President."

"Good night, Maria."

"Take care."

"See you tomorrow."

Soon Maria was alone in the room. But she didn't stay there long. She knew where she was going.

Picking up her purse, Maria headed for Joe Kent's store. She couldn't wait to tell Luis how well things had turned out at the meeting.

"Luis," she was saying to him in her mind, "if this can happen, anything can happen. You might really get to college. Why, who knows, I might even get to be a nurse. Anything can happen . . ."